Talking to Calippa
Cumberland

It began with a lost child on Christmas Eve

Chick Yuill

instant
apostle

First published in Great Britain in 2021

Instant Apostle
The Barn
1 Watford House Lane
Watford
Herts
WD17 1BJ

British Library Cataloguing-in-Publication Data

A catalogue record for this book is available from the British Library.

This book and all other Instant Apostle books are available from Instant Apostle:

Website: www.instantapostle.com

Email: info@instantapostle.com

ISBN 978-1-912726-48-6

Printed in Great Britain.

For the Son of Man came to seek and save the lost.

Luke 19:10

The Bible, New International Version

… the imagination becomes the privileged recipient
of divine inspiration …

Plato

A Dedication

This is a tale for anyone who has ever felt the
mysterious power of Christmas
to touch us and prompt us to tell stories of our own
that resonate with its Great Story.
It is a power I felt even while working on the
manuscript
in the middle of the heatwave that swept across the
United Kingdom in July 2021.
So this is my gift to you as the reader.
This is my Christmas story.
A story of loving and losing and finding.
A story of the child you and I once were and need to
become again.
A story to point us to the Child who is lost to us until
we allow him to find us.
A story to point us to the Child we all know even
when we get his name wrong.
A story to point us to the Child in whom we all can
confide.

It is also a gift to three very special women –
Mops, Shiney and Spenky.
You know who you are!
I offer it in deep gratitude for all you mean to me.
But it also comes with a heartfelt apology
for all the times when I've been less than
fully attentive
to the beauty, the blessings and the burdens you each
carry as a woman
in a world of often inattentive and sometimes even
uncaring men.
I'm learning. I mean to do better. And I love you.
CY

1
Christmas Eve 1976
We have a little girl here...

The visit to Santa's Grotto on Christmas Eve is an unexpected treat. Daddy will be coming home later this evening. Mummy has explained to me more than once that the reason Daddy has to be away from home so often and for such long periods is that 'he's earning the pennies for us to spend'. I miss him when he's away, but I like having the pennies. And I like it even more when he does come home, usually bringing something nice for me. And my excitement at the prospect of his return is always all the greater at Christmas time.

Mummy has decided at the last minute that she needs to buy him one more present, and my reward for being patient and well behaved while she searches for the perfect gift is to take my place in the queue of children waiting to tell Santa what they hope to find in their stockings tomorrow morning. It's been carefully explained to me more than once that this isn't the *real* Santa Claus. He, of course, is much too busy loading up his sleigh and harnessing the reindeer in preparation for his long night's work. This is simply one of his helpers enlisted to meet and talk with the line of eager girls and boys to find out what they're hoping for on Christmas morning and to ensure that the one true Santa will deliver the right presents to the right houses. It seems a plausible enough explanation, though I'm often puzzled as to why he has to wear exactly the same clothes as the genuine bearer of the title and consequently raise confusing questions in the minds of young children like me. Why doesn't he dress like one of the elves that I've seen in some of my books toiling all the live-long day in the toy-making workshop at the North Pole? Or at least he could wear a big badge saying, 'I'm not the real Santa. I'm just a helper.'

But they are questions that I'm happy to put to the back of my mind when – even more unexpectedly – my mother buys me my very first watch with the assurance that it isn't one of my Christmas presents and the promise that I can take it out of its box and wear it as soon as we get home. Such a prospect puts me in a state of excitement that almost takes my breath away. I've only just learned how to tell the time and I never miss an opportunity to impress anyone who's willing to listen with my newly acquired skill.

And that's why I remember so clearly the moment when I first become aware of the friend who, one way or another, will be with me for the rest of my life. I catch sight of the enormous clock with the gold lettering that hangs from the ceiling of Kendrew's Department Store. The big hand is on the 6 and the little hand is between the 4 and the 5.

'That means that it must be half past four,' I announce triumphantly and a little more loudly than my mother deems proper for a well-brought-up child from a family with aspirations to climb to the next rung of the social ladder.

'Well done,' she says taking hold of my hand and ushering me on to the downward escalator. 'But we don't need to tell all these people. I expect they already know how to tell the time for themselves.'

That seems a silly thing to say. Of course, they all know how to tell the time. Isn't that something everyone has to learn when they are children? I can't understand why she even bothers to mention it. But then, even at the age of three and three-quarters, I've already noticed that grown-ups, who seem to know such a lot, can still say silly things. When she thinks I'm misbehaving, Mummy will often look at me disapprovingly and say very quietly and slowly, 'You're forgetting yourself, Lori Bloom.' That's *really* silly. How could anybody forget themselves? You wouldn't know who you were or what you were doing or where you were going if you forgot yourself.

I'm still trying to work that out in my head when I realise that what I can hear coming through the speakers all around us is the sound of a man with a soft, gentle voice singing about things coming to pass when a baby is born. I can't understand why, but it's a song that always makes me feel sad and happy at the same time, though it seems to be about another silly thing. Why would things come just to pass and not to stay? It doesn't make sense to me, but my mother likes that song. She's been listening to it on the radio a lot. One afternoon I asked her what it meant. But she was doing something in the kitchen at the time and said she'd explain it to me when she wasn't so busy. It

11

occurs to me now that no one can be busy just standing on an escalator. So this should be a good time to ask her again.

But just as I'm about to speak, the music stops and I hear a very different voice. One that sounds serious, just like Daddy does when he thinks something is wrong with his car:

WE HAVE A LITTLE GIRL HERE WITH CURLY BLONDE HAIR AT RECEPTION. SHE'S CRYING FOR HER MUMMY AND DADDY. WOULD THE PARENTS OF…

'Lori, pay attention to what you're doing!' Mummy shouts and quickly grabs hold of my hand as the escalator steps level out and we reach the ground floor of the store. 'You'll fall if you don't watch out. You know I'm always telling you to be careful when you're on an escalator.'

'But, Mummy, a little girl is lost,' I protest. 'And you were talking to me when the man said her name. Shouldn't we go and find out who she is? Maybe we could wait with her until her mummy and daddy get there? What if they've forgotten her and gone home? Or what if they've decided they don't want her any more?'

My own safety is of no consequence to me compared to the situation of a little girl who is lost in a busy shop on Christmas Eve without her parents. I can imagine the panic she must be feeling as she struggles to stop herself from crying and tries to tell her name to some grown-ups she doesn't know.

'No, Lori, we're *not* going to reception.'

It's obvious from my mother's voice that she's irritated by my question and that she's not about to give in to my pleas. She's weary of shopping and all she wants to do is to get home as quickly as possible.

'We've been here longer than I intended as it is. And anyhow, the security people will have everything in hand. I'm sure her mummy and daddy will have missed her. They'll have been to reception and collected her before we could get there.'

She holds my hand tightly as she strides towards the revolving doors and out on to the street. I'm having to run to keep up with her as we hurry through the crowds. The damp chill of the evening serves only to increase my childish sense of injustice. Not even the brightly decorated shop windows or the colourful illuminations strung across the road above our heads can lift my mood. *A little girl is lost and we're doing nothing to help.* Just to go home and forget about it doesn't feel right.

It's almost six o'clock when we pull up into the driveway. The stop–start journey through the evening rush hour traffic has made me feel travel sick and I'm glad to get out of the car. I begin to feel better as soon as I get into the cold night air, and by the time we step through the front door I'm already feeling hungry. But I know we won't be having dinner until Daddy arrives home in another hour. So, at Mummy's suggestion, I help myself to a banana from the fruit bowl and go up to my room to try on my new watch.

My hunger is quickly forgotten and my banana is left uneaten as I fall under the spell of this newly acquired treasure. I handle it gently as I ease it slowly and carefully out of the box and put it on my wrist. It looks even nicer than it did in the shop. The strap is pink, the big hand is blue, the little hand is red, the face is white, and the numbers around the edge are green and orange and sparkly. I think that it's one of the prettiest things I've ever seen.

Normally, just admiring such a thing of beauty and playing games that involve pretending to be grown up and checking the time would keep me fully occupied for the rest of the evening. But even my unexpected not-Christmas present isn't enough to distract me from the thoughts that are troubling me. Try as I might to lose myself in the world of play, I can't get the picture of that lost little girl out of my mind. In my imagination I can see her curly blonde hair falling over her face and the tears rolling down her cheeks as she looks up into the eyes of people she doesn't know who are standing over her. Worst of all, I can hear her asking for her mummy over and over and over again.

I must have been lost in such thoughts for more than half an hour when I hear the front door open. I know exactly what that means and I rush downstairs. Daddy's home! He's standing there waiting for me when I reach the hallway. Even as a child I know that he's the most handsome man I've ever seen. And I've heard some of Mummy's friends tell her that with his thick, black, wavy hair and his deep blue eyes, her husband looks like a male model or a film star. As soon as he sees me, he drops his bag on the floor and I jump up into his arms.

'Well, well, well,' he says, holding me up above his head and noticing what I have on my wrist. 'We have a little girl here wearing a very posh new watch...'

He throws me up in the air and he's about to say something else as he catches me again. But I won't let him continue.

'No, stop, Daddy!' I shout. 'Put me down! Put me down!'

Mummy has a very cross expression on her face.

'Lori Bloom, that's not a nice way for a little girl to speak to her daddy. He's had a long journey so he could get home to be with us in time for Christmas. You need to say sorry. Right now.'

Every time I think of that moment it reminds me of a day trip we made to the seaside the previous summer. I was paddling in shallow water, looking at people sitting on the beach, when a big wave that I couldn't see came up behind me and knocked me off my feet. I'd never been completely under water before and I thought I was going to drown. I'm not a child who cries a lot, but when I try to say sorry to my daddy, a great wave of tears hits me and I can't stop crying. I feel as if I'm drowning in those deep, wrenching sobs. Daddy picks me up again, very gently this time, and carries me into the lounge where he sits me down on his knee.

'Now what's all this about, eh? It's not like you to get upset and cry like this. Especially on Christmas Eve. What's happened?'

The tears slowly begin to subside and then it all tumbles out – coming down on the escalator at Kendrew's, the man with the soft, gentle voice singing the song about a child being born and things coming to pass that always makes me feel sad and happy at the same time, the voice that interrupts the song with the message about the lost little girl.

'The man said the same words that you said just now, Daddy – *We have a little girl here...* That made me remember it all over again. That's what made me cry...'

I start crying all over again, but Daddy pulls out his big white handkerchief from his pocket, dries my eyes, and makes me blow my nose so loudly that the three of us laugh. The storm has passed and the wave has receded.

After dinner, Mummy clears the table and I go into the front room with Daddy. The room is in darkness except for the lights on the Christmas tree and the flickering flames in the log fire that make pretty changing patterns on the opposite wall. It's only the second Christmas I can properly remember, but already this has become in my mind 'what we always do on Christmas Eve'. We snuggle up together on the couch and I imagine I'm in an enchanted cavern where something magical might happen at any moment. It feels safe and warm and I want to stay there forever.

'I think you're falling asleep, Miss Lori.' Mummy's come back into the room. 'Come on. It's time for you to help me put some food out for Santa and then you must get off to bed. You know he doesn't visit a house unless the children are fast asleep.'

We go into the kitchen and set out a tray with a mince pie and a glass of milk, cover them with a bright red serviette, and lay a little card on top with the words, 'Thank you for coming, Santa,' written in gold-coloured ink. Then we go back into the front room so that I can kiss Daddy goodnight. He's just put a record on the radiogram and the music is beginning to play as we push the door open. It's the man with the soft gentle voice again, singing that same song about things coming to pass when a child is born. For a moment I think I'm back on the downward escalator at Kendrew's Department Store. But there's something else I can hear in my head. Something I haven't been able to remember until now.

'Turn the music off, Daddy! Please turn it off.' I'm half-crying, half-shouting, afraid that if the song doesn't stop the voice I can hear in my head will disappear and I'll forget it all over again. 'There's something else I remember…'

I didn't know the word for it then, but I'm looking up at two grown-ups who are utterly *bemused* by my anxious pleas. Daddy looks at Mummy, walks across the room to the radiogram and leans over and lifts the needle off the record.

'What's wrong, Lori?' he asks. 'Why don't you want the music to play?'

'Because I think I *did* hear what the man said in the shop when the song stopped. Mummy was telling me to be careful on the escalator. So it made me confused. But I think I really did hear what he said. I think I know the name of the little girl who's lost.'

'Hmm… you'd better come and sit down for a minute and tell us what you think you heard.'

Mummy sits on the couch beside me and Daddy kneels on the floor in front of me with his hands on my shoulders.

'Well, we're listening. What did you hear?'

'I think that the little girl's name is…' I pause for a moment to make sure I've got it right. 'I think it's *Calippa Cumberland.*'

Mummy and Daddy glance at each other again. Daddy leans back on his knees, folds his arms and rocks backwards and forwards for a moment. He looks at me over his eyebrows like he always does when he thinks I'm making up a story.

'*Calippa*? Hmm… that's a funny name. I don't think I've ever heard of anyone called *Calippa.* Are you sure you're not just making it up?'

'And maybe you're thinking of when we stayed with Uncle Rob and Auntie Cheryl in Cumberland Cottage last summer,' Mummy quickly adds with a smile. 'I seem to remember you liked the sound of the name. I think Daddy even made up a little song as you were going to sleep about being in slumberland in Cumberland.'

'No, no. I promise you I'm not making this up.' I can feel the tears beginning to well up again. 'I could *sort of* hear what the man was saying. I just couldn't work it out right in my head because you were talking at the same time. But that *is* her name. I'm sure it is. *Calippa Cumberland.* And maybe she's still there…'

Now there's no holding back the tears. I sob bitterly for a little lost girl all alone in Kendrew's Department Store on Christmas Eve after everyone else has gone home.

Daddy lifts me up and holds me tightly in his arms. He waits until my tears have subsided before he whispers in my ear.

'Listen to me very carefully, Lori. I'm going to take you up to bed now. I think you're very tired and you've had more than enough excitement for one day. And you need to be wide awake in the morning. So when we've tucked you up in bed I'll phone the police and ask if any little girls have been reported missing. And I'll call Kendrew's, just in case there's someone still there closing up the shop. I'm sure they'll tell me that the little girl was collected and taken home by her parents. So you can stop worrying about Miss Calippa Cumberland. Does that make you feel better?'

I half-mumble, half-yawn a tired yes and nod my head against his chest.

'Good,' he says as he begins carrying me upstairs. 'Now you can fall asleep and have lovely dreams about what will be waiting for you in the morning.'

But children are often wiser and understand more than grown-ups realise. I know that these are the kinds of promises parents make to their children to stop them from worrying. And I know that he will neither phone the police nor call the shop. As Mummy pulls back the covers and Daddy tucks me into bed, I've already made up my mind. Calippa Cumberland is lost in Kendrew's Department Store and no one will ever find her. She's doomed to wander unnoticed by busy shoppers day after day and to huddle in dark corners for warmth each night. But she won't be alone. I'll be her friend.

While every other child in England that Christmas Eve is dreaming of what delights the morning will bring, I'm talking to a little girl with curly blonde hair, helping her to dry her eyes and telling her not to be afraid because I will always be her friend.

2
Christmas Eve 1982
This isn't a Christmas card…

I've been hoping for the kind of day that's been imprinted on my mind for the last couple of weeks. The kind of day that's depicted on the cards that are strung across the walls of our front room – clear blue skies, a thick covering of snow on the ground from the previous night, and groups of smiling people in excited conversation, all of them wrapped up in scarves and thick woollen sweaters to protect them from the cold. The kind of day my father calls 'a proper Christmas Eve'. It is, however, cloudy and mild. And the warm coat and scarf I insisted on wearing when I went out to make the short walk to my schoolfriend Colette's house that morning are making me feel uncomfortably hot and sticky.

But neither my disappointment at the weather nor my regret that I haven't heeded my mother's advice to dress more appropriately can dampen my spirits as I skip the quarter of a mile down Newman Hill on my way home. It isn't just that it's Christmas Eve. Our house on Morley Road looks straight up the hill, so I can see it as soon as I say goodbye to Colette and set off. The sight of it drawing ever closer and looming larger with every step I take always gives me a surge of anticipation that I can still feel all these years later.

We moved to Morley Road from a nondescript new-build on the outskirts of Bristol when I was five. It's nearer to the upmarket boutique in the city centre where my mother works a couple of days each week. Equally importantly, Corton Primary is less than a twenty-minute walk from the house. It has a good reputation and my parents decided it would be the perfect school for their only child, a decision that turned out to be the right one for several reasons. I love the school, I love the neighbourhood, but I love that Victorian terraced house most of all.

On sunny days the Bath stone walls glow with a rich buff colour that allows me to imagine I'm living in a castle built of gold. Even on this dull day the house still looks impressively regal. Sitting confidently at the bottom of the hill behind its five-foot-high retaining wall that protects the raised garden, it has an imposing air of permanence and stability. And the four-panelled tall bay windows looking out from both the downstairs and upstairs rooms seem to survey everything in front of them and offer the assurance that no one will ever pass or enter unnoticed.

Number 17 Morley Road is a place of safety and shelter; within whose walls I'm sure that no bad thing can reach or harm me. And as I climb the five steps that lead up to the path, I can see the little fir tree that my mother and I planted in the front garden last year. This year we've decorated it with lights that are twinkling in the afternoon gloom. It makes the welcome the house always gives me all the greater.

I open the front door and let myself in. The old station waiting room clock that my Uncle Rob found at an auction and gave me as a surprise Christmas present last year is ticking loudly and showing that the time is exactly quarter to three. It would have been an entirely unsuitable and unwelcome gift for most eight-year-old girls, but it's a source of inexhaustible delight to a child who's been fascinated by such things ever since she learned to tell the time and lost her heart to the watch with the pink plastic strap and the green and orange sparkly numbers in Kendrew's Department Store at the age of three and three-quarters. I pleaded for it to be hung from its heavy black chain in the entrance porch where it can be seen and hopefully admired by everyone who calls at our house.

'Lori, is that you?' My mother is calling from the kitchen from where the sound of the radio and the smell of her cooking are filling the house and reaching the front door. 'Did you have a good time with your friend? I've left today's post for you to open. It's only Christmas cards, I think. You can bring them through and read them to me. Then we should get them hung up before your dad gets home.'

I kick off my shoes and hang up my coat and scarf before picking up the half dozen cards that are lying in the hallway and taking them through to the kitchen, where I put them on the little table in front of the serving hatch.

'Come on, then,' my mother says, feigning impatience as she slides another tray of biscuits into the oven. 'We didn't send you to school to learn to read just for you to sit and look at them. And you can turn the radio down so I can hear you properly.'

I do as she's instructed. I don't like the song she's listening to, especially since it seems to be on all the time. I've seen the two people on television – a man with very black hair and a big tummy bulging out of his jacket singing to a pretty lady with long blonde hair and a red dress who is standing on a balcony and singing back to him over and over again that he should save his love for her. I think it's really mushy and I can't see what it has to do with Christmas. It just seems to be another one of those silly things that grown-ups sometimes do. So I'm happy to turn the radio off and sit down at the table to read the Christmas cards.

The first three are from people still living in our old neighbourhood with whom we keep in touch. My mother suggests a little cynically that they've probably written them at the last minute, having forgotten to send us a card until they received ours a few days ago. There's one from someone whose signature we can't read and another from a distant relative in Australia. The last one has no stamp or postmark. And there's no street name or number. Just my mother's name 'Angela Bloom' written in pencil on the envelope. I show it to her with a quizzical look.

'Must be from one of the neighbours. They've decided just to pop it through the door and save the postage,' my mother says, shrugging her shoulders. 'Can't say I blame them for that. It can get expensive at this time of year.'

'It feels heavier than the others,' I say as I begin to open it. 'Maybe they've spent the money they saved on stamps and put it to one of those really expensive cards...'

I hold the envelope with the sealed edge between my thumb and forefinger and shake it gently to let the card slide on to the table. But there is no card. What falls out are five black-and-white photographs – photographs of people sitting round tables with drinks in front of them, people who look as if they're enjoying themselves – and a piece of paper folded in four. Just like the envelope, it has my mother's name, Angela Bloom, written on it in pencil. I think it's odd that Daddy is in all the photographs sitting beside a woman I don't recognise. On one of them he has his arm round the woman and on another one he's kissing her. That one really puzzles me. He's kissing her, not like Uncle Rob kisses Mummy on the cheek when he and Auntie Cheryl come to visit us, but on the lips like men and women do when they're married or in love with each other.

'This isn't a Christmas card,' I say, unsure why I'm beginning to feel nervous, like I do when I think that something unpleasant or scary is about to happen. 'There's just some photos of Daddy at a party. And there's this letter with your name on it, Mummy.'

My mother has just washed her hands and is reaching for a towel lying at the end of the worktop.

'Oh, they're probably the photos from the night last month when we met up with the Halls and the Martins for drinks and nibbles. Why don't you read the letter to me while I finish what I'm doing? I can't think it's anything too private.'

My hands are trembling as I unfold the sheet of A4 paper and begin to read the handwritten message.

Angela Bloom you need to know your husband is a piece of …

There's a word that I'm never allowed to say at home. Why would someone write that word about my daddy? I feel like I always do when something unexpected happens that frightens me. My heart is bumping in my chest. I stop reading and push the piece of paper away from me.

'Mummy, I don't think this is a very nice letter. I don't want to read it.'

My mother puts down the towel and asks me to hand her the letter. Apart from the low humming sound from the oven everything seems to become suddenly quiet. My mother stands very still and I can hear her breathing slowly and deeply while she reads it.

'Something's wrong, Mummy, isn't it?' I ask anxiously. 'Has Daddy done something bad?'

She folds the letter up and slips it in the pocket on the front of her apron.

'No, no,' she says, shaking her head. 'No, I'm sure your daddy hasn't done anything wrong. There's nothing for you to worry about. It's just a nasty letter from someone who doesn't like him and is trying to cause trouble. Let's not mention this to Daddy when he gets home. I'll talk to him about it tonight after you've gone to bed. But you mustn't think about it any more.'

She's smiling at me reassuringly, but I'm not sure whether I should believe her. I need to think. I need to talk to somebody who never fails to listen. So I do what I regularly do when I need to sort things out in my head. Sometimes it's when I'm really happy about something; sometimes it's when I have a secret I want to share with someone; and sometimes, like at this moment, it's when things are troubling me.

I go back to the hallway, put my shoes on again and go out through the side door to the stretch of grass at the back of the house. Mummy sometimes looks at it wistfully from the kitchen window and remarks that it could look much better if Daddy wasn't so reluctant to have a gardener. For some reason that I can't understand, he doesn't like having people that he doesn't know in and around the house.

It's easy to clamber up onto the low stone wall that separates us from our next-door neighbour's rather more cared-for garden. The top of the wall is wide enough and flat enough for me to walk back and forth on it safely without falling off. That's where I often go to talk to the person who I know will be waiting for me. A little girl whose blonde curls contrast with my own long, straight, thick, black hair. Calippa Cumberland has been my frequent companion ever since that Christmas Eve six years ago when I helped her dry her eyes, told her not to be afraid and promised her that I would be her friend.

My parents weren't too concerned when they first became aware of what they called my 'fixation' with Calippa. They expected it to wear off after a month or two. When it persisted through the spring and into the summer of 1982, they took me to see our GP who recommended that I have an appointment with Dr Edith Barker, a psychologist who specialised in working with children. I really liked her. Unlike most of the grown-ups I knew, she listened more than she talked, and when she did speak to me she treated me like an equal. She understood what I meant when I explained to her that Calippa Cumberland was *really real*, but not in the same way that Sarah Tattersall, my best friend at school, was real.

'I know what you mean,' she said with a twinkle in her eye after we talked about it for a little while. 'I had a friend like Calippa when I was your age. Sometimes, when I have things I need to talk about, we still have a little chat with each other.'

She was able to assure my anxious parents that it wasn't particularly unusual for a child of my age to have an imaginary friend. And, even though my friendship with Calippa had had an unusual beginning, she was confident that there was no cause for alarm. Her opinion was that I was probably of above-average intelligence, and that I certainly wasn't in need of any further professional medical help.

'Your daughter's quite healthy and well,' she said as she returned me to my parents after our conversation. 'Many children make up stories to help them make sense of things. And for some it goes a bit further than that and one of the characters in their story takes on a kind of life of their own and becomes an imaginary friend, just like Calippa. I've got a colleague who also writes novels and he tells me that something similar still happens to him when he's writing. He creates a character who then seems to assume a life of their own, does something my colleague never expected, and takes the story he's writing in a completely unexpected direction. There's nothing spooky or mystical about it. And certainly nothing to worry about in my experience. Just seems to be all part of the creative ability of the human mind. Imagination's a powerful thing and not to be feared.'

If my parents weren't fully persuaded by Dr Barker's explanation, it did at least set their minds at rest sufficiently for them to resist the urge to banish Calippa Cumberland from the family.

And now, in the late afternoon of Christmas Eve, there's just enough light coming from the kitchen window for me to see where I'm stepping, though I've walked backwards and forwards on this wall so many times that I could do it with my eyes closed. And just as always happens, I begin to see things a little more clearly as I talk with Calippa. To anyone who might overhear our 'conversations', they would sound one-sided, to say the least. Nothing more than a child with a vivid imagination talking to herself, asking and answering her own questions in a semi-whisper. But for me, they are significant encounters with a friend whose solitude and seclusion have given her a unique perspective on life and made her wise beyond her years. Her cruel abandonment by her parents has made her an acute observer of everything around her. And what began for me as a surge of sympathy for a little lost girl with fair skin and curly blonde hair has become a regular encounter with a friend who helps me to puzzle things out and find my way through a confusing world in which adults who know a lot often say silly things and seldom have the time to listen properly to a child.

By the time I get down from the wall and go back indoors, I feel sure that my fears are justified and that Daddy *has* done something bad. There's a lot that I don't understand about the differences between men and women and what attracts them to each other. I know that

I don't like boys very much and it's a mystery to me why older girls are so keen to impress them and get them to like them. But I understand enough to be sure that the kind of kisses my father was giving to the woman in those photographs should be saved just for my mother. And I also understand that it's best not to say anything. My mother is determined that nothing should spoil our Christmas together and I know that I have to go along with that.

I'm putting my shoes on the rack in the hallway and changing into my slippers when I hear the key turn in the lock behind me. The door swings open and my father drops his bag on the floor just as he always does when he arrives home. He reaches down to me and lifts me up into his arms.

'There's my girl,' he says as he carries me through to the kitchen. 'Goodness me, you're getting bigger every time I come home. Soon you'll be a young lady and you won't want me to hug you like this. I'd better take the chance while I still can.'

Something inside me recoils from him and I have to resist an urge to wriggle out of his arms and tell him that I don't want to him to hug me. Not now. Not ever again. I feel overwhelmed by a confusing mixture of emotions that I'd never experienced before and I'm glad when he sits me down on a chair and throws his arms around my mother. He has his back to me, and my mother is facing me with her head on his shoulder as they embrace each other. My face must be showing an expression of anger or revulsion of which I'm unaware because my mother is looking at me very hard. Her eyes narrow and she gives a tiny but unmistakable shake of her head. I know exactly what she means by that.

We sit around the kitchen table at half past six to eat supper. Ever since I've been old enough to enjoy spicy food and decide that it's my favourite, we always have *chilli con carne* on Christmas Eve. But this year it doesn't seem to have its usual taste.

'You haven't got much of an appetite this evening, Lori,' my father says as he looks at my still half-full plate. 'You always tell us how much you like this one. Are you feeling alright? You're not sickening for something, are you?'

I shake my head and make the excuse that I had a big lunch at Colette's house and I'm still not hungry.

'I expect you tucked into too many sweets as well,' my mother says.

It's obvious to me that she knows the truth about what's affecting my appetite and that she's coming to my aid by giving me an excuse. I immediately agree with her. But she and I both know that I'm lying.

'I'm OK, but I don't think I'll stay up too late tonight. I'm a little bit tired and I want to be wide awake for the morning.' I'm trying to think of something that won't make it look too obvious that I just want to be on my own. I pick on another one of our family traditions on Christmas Eve. 'Maybe we could play just one game of Scrabble and then I'll go to bed.'

'That's an excellent idea,' my mother responds enthusiastically. 'Why don't you go and set it up on the table in the front room while Daddy and I clear the supper things away and tidy up the kitchen?'

It takes me only a few minutes to get the board out of the box, put the three little wooden racks around it and make sure all the tiles with the letters on them are safely in the velvet bag. It seems to take a long time for my mother and father to join me. And the longer I wait, the more nervous I become. What if they're talking about those photographs right now? What if they're having an argument and my mother's crying? It's a relief when they come into the room smiling and chatting to each other.

Despite the appearance of everything being normal, neither my mother nor I are able to concentrate on the game.

'Well, I don't know what's wrong with you two this evening,' my father says with a triumphant smile as he puts down his last letter and tots up the scores. 'But you didn't put up much of a fight. So I win that one easily. D'you want to play another game and see if either of you can do any better?'

My mother makes the excuse that she needs to finish off some preparation for tomorrow's Christmas dinner and I remind them both that I'm tired and want to go to bed early.

'Well, I guess I'll just have to sit and watch television on my own with a glass of something nice,' my father says, feigning tears. '*The Stanley Baxter Hour*'s on ITV. I like him. He's really funny. But you need to give me a goodnight kiss, Lori, before you head for your room.'

My mother often describes me as 'a daddy's girl'. And she's right. I love him. I love the presents he brings me every time he comes home from one of his business trips. I love his thick black hair that he allows me to comb when

I'm pretending to be a hairdresser. I love the silly jokes he tells that make me chuckle even when I try not to laugh. I love his big strong arms when he picks me up and carries me. I love the manly smell of his aftershave that seems so grown-up and sophisticated. I love the way the stubble on his face tickles me when he gives me a kiss. But tonight I cringe as he holds me close to him. And I know instinctively that something precious has been damaged that will not be easily repaired.

I climb the stairs to my bedroom, trying without success to understand my emotions. Things are just as they've always been on Christmas Eve. The holly wreath is hanging on the front door. Daddy is sitting watching television with a glass of wine in his hand. Mummy is pottering around in the kitchen and listening to the radio as she finishes off the last-minute preparations for our Christmas dinner. The cards are strung along the walls of the front room. And the brightly lit tree is standing in the corner with presents for all three of us piled underneath. But Christmas Eve never felt like this before. Those photographs that fell on to the table and that nasty letter I started to read have changed everything and I can't make sense of it at all.

I close the bedroom door quietly behind me, relieved to be on my own again. In a house that I've come to believe is strong enough to shut out anything that might harm me, this is the safest and happiest place of all. The duvet cover on my bed and the wallpaper on all four walls are printed with a matching pattern of lavishly coloured rainbows and fluffy white clouds floating in a perfectly clear blue sky. On the wall opposite my bed there is an old, black, cast-iron fireplace. Every time I look at it, I remember that this is an *old* house. And as the latest occupant of this room, I'm just one character in a long story that's much bigger than me, a story that reaches back into a distant past, a story that will continue into an unknown future long after I've grown up and gone to live in a house of my own. It's more than a room where I come to be alone, to read in the day and to sleep at night. It's a secret chamber not just at the top of our house, but at the top of the world; a hideaway in which time stands still; a portal through which I have access to a realm in which everything I can imagine might easily become reality; a place that for now belongs only to me and whoever I invite to enter.

I lie on my bed and wish that life could go on unchanged. Why can't things just stay like they've always been? A few hours ago, everything was fine. *It's Christmas Eve.* Daddy is home for a few days before going off on his travels again, and we're a complete family. Now everything feels uncertain.

The book I was reading earlier is lying on the little table beside my bed. So I open it and try to pick up the story where I left off, but I can't concentrate and the words just get jumbled up in my head. There's nothing else to do but to get ready for bed. I get undressed, put on my pyjamas, go to the bathroom and brush my teeth, and then try to settle down for the night.

I've always had difficulty falling asleep on Christmas Eve, but that's because I've been so excited about what surprises awaited me in the morning. Now I can't sleep for a very different reason. *I'm afraid.* If the person I've loved and trusted most in all the world has been telling lies and cheating like the letter said, I don't know if I can trust anyone ever again.

Since I can't think of anything else to do, I get out of bed, go over to the window and pull back the curtains. I can see all the way to the top of Newman Hill and I wish I could turn the clock back to when I set off from Colette's house earlier in the day. Maybe I would arrive home and there would be no puzzling photographs and no nasty letter.

The sound of someone tapping gently on my bedroom door brings me back into the moment.

'Lori, are you alright?' My mother is speaking in a whisper as she slips quietly into the room. 'I thought I heard you moving around. I don't want you to be worrying about anything.'

She closes the door very quietly behind her and beckons to me to sit beside her on the bed. She gives me a look that tells me she's well aware of what I've been thinking about and why I've taken myself off to bed early.

'Daddy's dropped off to sleep in front of the television, but he and I have talked about the photographs and he's explained it all to me.' She's smiling and patting me on the leg as she speaks. 'And there's absolutely nothing for you to worry about. It was just a silly game they were playing at his office party and one of the forfeits was that they had to kiss someone who was wearing something black. He didn't want to do it, but everyone else insisted he had to follow the rules of the game. He doesn't really know the lady in the picture and he can't even remember her name. She's only been with the firm a few months. And, of course, he's travelling such a lot that he's hardly ever in the office here in Bristol. He thinks the person who put the envelope through our letter box is someone who used to work with him, someone he had to give a telling-off and who had to leave because they weren't doing their job very well. So it sounds as if it's someone who's just trying to be unkind and get her own back on Daddy.'

She gets up and walks over to the window. She stands and looks out for a moment before she draws the curtains shut again.

'Come on, let's get you into bed.' She tucks the duvet around me, strokes my hair gently and gives me a kiss on my forehead. 'Now, promise me that you won't do any more worrying. You must try to forget what you saw and have a good night's sleep. Lots of surprises waiting for you in the morning, remember.'

'I promise you,' I nod. 'And I'll try not to think about it ever again.'

'Good.' She pauses at the bedroom door and turns back to me. 'And just one more thing. I haven't told Daddy that you saw the photographs. He'd be really upset at the thought of you being troubled in any way. So it's best not to mention it to him at all. OK?'

I nod my head against my pillow and she winks at me knowingly before tiptoeing out of the room and closing the door quietly behind her. As I drift off to sleep, I'm vaguely aware of music coming from the radio in the kitchen where my mother must be doing some last-minute preparation. It's that song again. The tubby man is singing to the pretty lady that she should save her love for him...

3
Christmas Eve 1986
There's a time to stop pretending...

I must have been standing by the window looking up Newman Hill for almost a quarter of an hour. I'm not looking at anything in particular. Quite the opposite, in fact. I'm just staring straight ahead, thinking about how empty the road seems, thinking about what I *won't* see this afternoon. I *won't* see my father's black sports car coming down the hill at a speed that always scares the life out of my mother, spinning around and stopping with a screech in front of the house. I *won't* see him easing himself out of the low driver's seat and yawning as he stretches to ease the stiffness from his limbs after his journey from whatever part of the country he's come from. And I *won't* see him striding up the path with a grin on his face, a couple of expensively wrapped presents tucked under one arm, and his bag swinging from his other hand. Not this Christmas Eve. Not for years to come.

I turn and look over my shoulder to check the time on the old station waiting room clock behind me. I insisted on moving it from its prominent position in the hallway to be hung in my bedroom two days ago, after I was told about the sentence. My mother was adamant that moving it was a bad idea. Indeed, she'd have been happy if we'd got rid of the clock and dumped it at the recycling centre. She's always called it a monstrosity and says that the sight of it hanging above the black cast-iron fireplace opposite my bed makes the room look like a gloomy corner in a Victorian workhouse. It definitely isn't the kind of thing any teenager should have in their bedroom, she tells me with a despairing shake of her head. Besides which, she contends not unreasonably, its loud, ominous ticking might keep me awake at nights.

But I win in the end. And I know that the real reason for her reluctance to let me have my way isn't her unhappiness with the décor of my room, much as she dislikes that. It's her fear that my fascination with time, which began innocently enough with my sense of achievement at learning to read what was on a clock face and my childish pleasure in owning my first watch, is in danger of becoming an obsession.

Given the news of the last week, it's little wonder that my mind is even more preoccupied with thoughts about the slow passing of minutes and hours. My mother told me at the beginning of November that my father had to appear in court.

'It's just some technical stuff to do with his work for "the firm". Some regulations they've broken, I think. That kind of thing,' she explained. 'Nothing for us to concern ourselves with. He'll probably get fined. But it's best if you don't think about it. I know how much you love your

37

daddy. So I don't want you worrying and your schoolwork being affected.'

She's cancelled the newspaper order, turns off the television whenever the local news comes on, and made me promise that I won't try to find out what's happening. I'm in my second year at George Fulford College, a fee-paying school where my parents secured a place for me. The more I think about it, the more odd it seems to me that none of my teachers or fellow-pupils have made any mention of the court case. I can only guess that she's contacted the head teacher and made sure that she's enlisted the school in her conspiracy of silence. So when she told me just a week before Christmas that the judge had sentenced my father to five years in prison I was too shocked even to cry.

'But he hasn't hurt anyone or done anything really bad,' I protested angrily. 'I know he's done something wrong, and I know he has to be punished for that. But why does he have to go to prison? Five years is such a long time. I'll be almost nineteen by the time they let him out.'

She tried to console me by explaining that most prisoners don't actually serve their full sentence and that they're usually released early, provided they behave themselves and keep to the rules while they're locked up. If he's lucky, she concluded, patting my hand, he could be out in three years. Her words were of little comfort to a thirteen-year-old whose thoughts are as confused and whose emotions are as conflicted as mine.

So much has happened since I dropped those photos out of the envelope on to the table and read the start of that letter four Christmases ago. At first everything seemed to be fine and things continued as they'd always done. If I'd been initially dubious of my mother's assurances that the whole thing was nothing more than an act of revenge by a former workmate with a score to settle, the strength of my desire for life to carry on as normal was enough to push those feelings deep below my conscious thought. I persuaded myself that my mother was right and that there really was nothing for me to worry about. After all, I was generally a happy child: I loved my parents, even though I resented my father's long absences; I had two good friends in Sarah and Colette, and I was excelling at my studies. And those 'pennies that daddy earned' provided us with luxuries that were denied to most children of my age. He still spent weeks away from us – 'on the road' was the phrase that was always used – and, as the months passed into years, his visits home became shorter and more sporadic until they amounted to little more than a day or two every five or six weeks. But my mother seemed at ease with the situation. And when I would ask her, 'Why does Daddy need to be away from home quite so much?' she would shrug her shoulders and tell me it was just how things were when someone did the kind of work he did. Exactly what that work was, neither of my parents were ever able or willing to explain to me.

'It's grown-up stuff,' my father would say with a laugh. 'Nothing you need to worry about. And anyhow, if I started to tell you what I do every day, you'd get really bored within two minutes. It's not really very interesting.'

All I knew was that it had something to do with his work for what we always called 'the firm'. I had a vague idea from snatches of conversation I'd overheard between my parents that 'the firm' was involved in the jewellery business. It had premises somewhere on the outskirts of Bristol, a place to which I went only once. But that solitary visit imprinted itself on my memory and was one of the things that began to make me feel that everything was not exactly as it seemed. I went there on the afternoon of my tenth birthday, three months after the arrival of that hand-delivered letter and the photos that had disturbed me. I was so excited about reaching what I proudly called my 'double digits' that I pleaded with him over the phone to come home and celebrate the day with us. He agreed only after much persuasion, promising to get to us in time for breakfast. He didn't arrive until after midday, and at half past two he had a telephone call from one of his colleagues at 'the firm' telling him that he had to pick up a package before he left. The call seemed to make him suddenly anxious, and he decided that he needed to collect whatever it was immediately.

'There's no point in me coming back after that,' he said apologetically as he picked up his car keys. 'So I'll head straight back from there.'

He beckoned to me to come and give him a kiss, but I was having none of it. I was so distraught at the thought of him leaving early that I threw a tantrum.

'You hardly ever come to see Mummy and me,' I sobbed, 'and now you're not even going to stay long enough for my birthday tea. I've been really excited about you being here. But you don't care about me. I hate you!'

I wasn't a child who got easily upset and my outburst took him by surprise. There were furtive glances and a whispered conversation between my parents, and eventually they agreed that I should go with him and that, after he'd brought me back home, he'd stay for another hour so that we could celebrate my birthday properly.

'But you'll need to wait in the car for me while I pick up the package. It'll only take me a minute. And you mustn't get out of the car or talk to anyone. Do you understand? It's really important.'

I was so pleased to have got him to agree to stay a little longer that I readily agreed to his instructions, quickly wiped the tears from my eyes and got into the car with him.

When I think back to that day, I realise that it was one of only two or three occasions in my childhood that he and I ever went anywhere together – just the two of us. Throughout those years, even though his presence loomed large in my life, it was as if he was casting a long shadow from a great distance. But I adored him and I was delighted to have this opportunity to have my daddy all to myself. And it was all the sweeter because it would never have happened had I not reacted as I did a little earlier. It taught me that tears can sometimes be turned on to good effect.

We drove for about twenty minutes before we turned into a side street and pulled up outside what I would have guessed was an abandoned shop of some kind had it not been for the roll-down shutters covering the window and the heavy steel door. They were in obvious contrast to the peeling paint and crumbling stonework and looked as if they'd been fitted fairly recently.

My father got out of the car, looking first one way and then the other before warning me again not to open a window or speak to anyone as he locked the door behind him. I couldn't quite understand why he was so concerned for my safety. There was no one on the street as far as I could see. And yet, young as I was, I sensed that this wasn't the kind of area where anyone would want to be walking alone at any time of the day or night.

As he'd promised, he left me on my own for less than a minute. I watched him pressing a buzzer by the side of the door, which swung open almost immediately. He stepped quickly inside, leaving the door slightly ajar. A few seconds later he came back out and the noise of the steel door clanging shut echoed down the street. He looked up and down the street again, and then hurried back to the car with a wooden box under his arm. He put the box in the boot, got back into the car and we drove off at speed.

All the way home he kept telling me jokes and trying to make me laugh. I wanted to ask him what was in the box and why 'the firm' had its premises in such a drab part of the city. But I was old enough to pick up the signal from his overenthusiastic jesting. He was not about to answer my questions on where we had just been or on the nature of his work. It was not something he would ever talk about to me.

That was really the first time it began to dawn on me that our family had a secret. A secret my mother must have shared to some extent, even if she didn't know – or didn't care to know – all the details. Whatever it was that he did to 'earn the pennies' that provided for us, I realised that it must be different from the way in which the fathers of most of my classmates earned their living.

By the time we got back to Morley Road that afternoon, my mother had laid the table ready for my birthday tea, complete with a cake decorated to look like the face of the old station waiting room clock that I loved so much, with both hands pointing to the number ten. And there were presents for me that would have made most girls of my age green with envy. If a passer-by had been able to see us through one of those big windows at the front of the house, they might well have gone on their way envious of the small but happy family celebrating their daughter's birthday party. What they would never have imagined was that the person in whose honour the party had been arranged was struggling to stifle the troublesome thought that we were not quite the perfect family we appeared to be.

And now, as I turn away from the window, the old clock is telling me that it's half past three and the advent calendar above my bed is reminding me that it's Christmas Eve. Fifteen minutes have ticked away while I've been standing at the window thinking about how much life has changed since that birthday party in March 1983. And that's when I make the decision. I can't put it off any longer. I have to talk to my mother. I have to know the truth. It feels like a moment of sudden resolve. But there is also a vague sense that my decision comes from somewhere deep within me. From the physical and emotional changes taking place as the processes of puberty make themselves evident.

I was still only a child when the words in that handwritten letter fixed themselves in my memory: 'Angela Bloom you need to know your husband is a piece of …' I knew then that whoever had written them was talking about something that I understood only dimly. There was a big part of adult life that was still a mystery to me – a part that manifested itself in a constant stream of communication between men and women, communication that was conducted in a language I could not translate and reinforced by gestures and looks I could not interpret. I sensed that, more mysterious still to me, those words and signals were pointing to something far beyond the boundaries of any frame of reference I possessed.

But I've changed since then. My body has changed. I'm not just a child any longer. I'm becoming a woman. And I'm learning to cope with a new relentless monthly rhythm to my life and with the physical and emotional demands it's imposing on me. So this is what I've overheard older girls talking about. Whatever I'd imagined the word *period* to mean, it certainly wasn't this. There's been little conversation between my mother and me about such things beyond some basic hygiene instructions and her swift and easy dismissal of my tears and complaints about the discomfort I experience.

'Things will get easier as you get older,' she repeats glibly. 'There are worse things. And anyhow, there'll come a time when you'll just be grateful that it turns up every month. It's when it doesn't arrive that you'll have cause to be concerned.'

I'm not at all sure what could be worse than what to me is an unwelcome and unpleasant monthly attack on my body. But that kind of cold counsel, usually accompanied by coded warnings to be careful and not get 'carried away' in the company of boys, is the extent of our conversations on what it means to be growing up as a woman in a world where men seem to be in control. Sex education lessons at school are more helpful as far as they go, though they seem to be mainly focused on the messy mechanics of 'it' – that little one-syllable word is shorthand among the girls at school for anything related to the subject of sex – rather than helping us to discover what this strange, new dimension to our experience will mean for us as we go through life.

At the same time, and in complete contrast, I'm also waking up to the truth that boys can't be as easily ignored or discounted as they have been in the past. They're no longer just loud, annoying, sweaty creatures to be avoided at all costs. (Well, some are… And some seem unlikely ever to change for the better, whatever their age.) But there are others who've altered in a way that's bewilderingly different from and yet fascinatingly parallel to the transformation that's taking place in me. And I'm learning how just one brief look or a casual smile across the classroom from Johnny Barker can leave me confused by the power of my own emotions for the rest of the day.

Of course, there's still so much of which I know nothing. I've learned enough, however, to have a fair idea of what the writer of that letter might have been referring to. And in the last few weeks, even though I followed her instructions not to try to find out about the court case, I have seen that my mother has been becoming increasingly concerned about what's been happening. On the one occasion I raised the subject with her, she said only that she would tell me the outcome of the trial when a verdict had been delivered. And I can't help noticing that she doesn't resort to her customary justification of his actions as 'just the kind of work he's in and the way that companies like his sometimes have to do business'.

She remains unwilling to speak of it, telling me that there's nothing I need to be concerned about and that we'll be alright whatever happens. But I'm old enough to face the truth, not just about his criminal activities but also about what I'm beginning to suspect is the other unacknowledged reason for his prolonged absences.

It's Christmas Eve. But nothing can lighten my mood or hide the fact that there's a distinct absence of any festive cheer in our home. And as I close my bedroom door behind me and walk quietly downstairs, my mind is made up. I will not go to sleep tonight until I've found out the answers to my questions.

The house is filled with the same array of sights and sounds and smells that have marked every Christmas I can remember. As I pass the open door of the front room, I can see the tree festooned with lights and ornaments, glistening with tinsel and surrounded by presents of all shapes and sizes. Everything is just like it's been every year. Except that this year we won't have my father with us to play the role of Santa Claus with his customary flamboyance. But Uncle Rob and Auntie Cheryl will be joining us for Christmas and my mother is determined to make everything feel as normal as possible.

'Uncle Rob will do the honours this time. Well, it needs the sound of a man's voice to read the name tags and pass the gifts around,' she attempts to explain with a logic that I can't fathom as she sets the last parcel down under the tree. 'Wouldn't be right for a woman to do it. Just wouldn't feel like Christmas.'

Even a stranger, blindfolded and visiting the house for the first time, could find their way to the kitchen just by following the smells that come wafting from that direction – the unmistakable aroma of cakes that have been taken out of the oven less than five minutes ago and laid on a rack to cool. And, just as she always does when she's baking, my mother is listening to music on the radio. It's the sound of the current seasonal chart-topper – a song by the Housemartins asking if I'm ready for the time of my life.

Now that I'm a fully fledged teenager, I'm becoming ever more aware of pop culture. I even managed to impress some of my more streetwise classmates by singing along to the lyrics of the song at a school party on the last day of term. But whether what I'm about to do will prove to be the time of my life, and whether I'm really ready for it, I'm not sure. But I *am* certain that I can't put it off any longer.

'Mum, can we turn the radio down?' I answer my own question by switching it off completely. 'And can I talk to you? Please…'

A look of irritation flashes across her face. It's an expression I've seen whenever I try to ask her about my father's arrest. And increasingly over recent months she retreats to the sanctuary of her kitchen – usually with a glass of wine by her side and always with the radio on – where she loses herself in a frenzied round of cooking and baking. It seems to be the one place where she feels safe and in control. The one place where she can escape from a world she's finding increasingly difficult to cope with. A quick glance in our cupboards or in the freezer is enough to show that she's prepared and stored sufficient food to feed an army for weeks.

'I'm really busy right now,' she responds, distracted by what she still has to do and annoyed by my question. 'Uncle Rob and Auntie Cheryl will be arriving just after seven and there's still a lot to be done. I've got a bit more to finish in here. So I could do with you making up their bed and seeing that their room's ready for them when they get here. Anyhow, Christmas Eve isn't the time for conversations like you're thinking of.'

She turns away quickly, wiping away the tear that's started to trickle down her cheek with the back of her hand and pretending to consult the recipe book that's propped up on the wooden stand in front of her. For a moment I wonder if I should forget the whole thing and just put it off until another day. But I know there will never be a right time for our conversation. I can't let this opportunity pass.

'Mum, I finished off everything in their room this morning. So you don't need to worry about that. But we've *got* to talk before they get here. *There's a time to stop pretending.* I'm not a child and I'm not stupid. I've grown up. I'm thirteen and I'm old enough to know the truth. I want to know about Daddy's involvement with "the firm" – whatever that means. And I want to know about that letter and those photographs that you never want to talk about. Please stop what you're doing for ten minutes and talk to me.'

She stands with her back to me for almost a minute without speaking, one hand resting on the worktop and the other touching the open recipe book on the stand, as if she's trying to check for an ingredient she's missed or to work out why something she's just taken out of the oven has gone so wrong. When she does eventually turn towards me, I'm shocked at how she looks. She's suddenly changed in a way that frightens me. She's always gone to a great deal of trouble over her appearance. It doesn't matter if she's not going to leave the house all day. She still dresses immaculately and tastefully, choosing her wardrobe with all the care of a model getting ready for a photoshoot and never starting her day without taking at least half an hour to apply her make-up.

'A woman has to look good for her husband,' she'll tell me whenever I ask why she's being so fussy. And then she'll often add that, apart from it being her duty as a good wife, it's important for her to be at her best 'just in case anyone calls at the door unexpectedly'. Even when she's working in the kitchen, her apron will be perfectly laundered and ironed, selected from her considerable collection of cooking attire so as to complement her clothing. She is ever the perfect housewife. But now tears are flowing, her mascara is running in black streaks and her mouth is open. It's as if she's lost all control of her facial muscles.

'Mum, I'm sorry,' I say, taking her hand. 'I didn't mean to upset you. It's alright. We don't need to talk about it now if you really don't want to. Let's wait until after Christmas.'

She shakes her head slowly, easing her hand out of mine, and reaches for a piece of kitchen roll to wipe her eyes. Now her mascara is smudged all over her face. It makes her look like a sad circus clown. At any other time it would have made me laugh. Now I feel so sorry for her that I want to cry.

'No, you're right,' she says, crumpling up the piece of kitchen roll and throwing it in the bin. 'We *do* need to talk. I've been putting it off and that's not good. It's not just you that I've been pretending to. I've been pretending to myself. Just give me time to go upstairs and wash my face. You make me a cup of tea and we'll sit down and talk.'

She comes back in five minutes, having removed every trace of her make-up. Apart from first thing in the morning when she's just got out of bed, I can't remember her ever going about the house without 'putting my face on', as she always describes it. She looks drained and exhausted, more tired than I've ever seen her.

I'm about to pour the water from the kettle into her cup when she stops me with a wave of her hand.

'You know what, Lori? Don't bother with the tea.' She stoops down and reaches into the back of one of the cupboards under the worktop and draws out a bottle of wine. 'I think I need something just a little stronger than tea if I'm going to tell you what you need to know.'

She uncorks the bottle, fills the plastic beaker that's on the table and drinks from it like someone with a desperate thirst. When she puts it down, she has to clasp her hands together to stop them from trembling. It takes her a moment or two before she can begin to speak, and at first her words come slowly and quietly as she eases herself into the conversation by covering what is familiar ground to us both.

'Daddy's been involved in the jewellery business for as long as I've known him. I've told you about how he was a sales rep and how we met when he came into the jeweller's shop where I worked. He really was a very good-looking man. He still is. All the girls liked him, but for some reason he seemed to be particularly interested in me. I couldn't believe it when he asked me out. My dad left your grandma and me and Auntie Cheryl just after my third birthday and I wasn't all that confident around boys. And I wasn't one of the really popular girls at school. I was always kind of on the edge of things. So I was swept off my feet by his attention.'

She looks at me with a wistful smile that makes me wish I could have known her in those days. And for the first time it occurs to me that, though we are different in so many ways, we are more alike than I have realised. I know exactly what it's like to be 'on the edge of things', as she puts it.

I reach across and touch the back of her left hand. She puts her right hand on top of mine and squeezes it a little. It seems to give her the energy to carry on with her story.

'I was only nineteen when we got married. Not all that much older than you are now, in some ways. He'd only just turned twenty. Looking back, we were very young. But he'd been adopted when he was a baby and he'd never had a particularly happy relationship with the couple who'd adopted him. He wasn't quite seventeen when he walked out on them and he had to learn how to look after himself pretty quickly. I know he had a string of dead-end jobs and lived in cheap lodgings for a while. Then things seemed to change suddenly and almost overnight he started to make really good money for his age. I guess that's when he got involved with "the firm", though he never told me much about it other than that they spotted potential in him and gave him responsibility. Auntie Chery had already left home by the time my mum suddenly got sick and died, and I was left on my own. Daddy had moved into a nice apartment. So a month after Grandma's funeral we got married at the registrar's office in Montefiore Street. But you know all about all this already.'

I'm surprised when she reaches for the bottle again and refills the plastic beaker, swirling the wine around a couple of times before she takes another mouthful. I've never seen her drink more than one glass of wine, and then only on an evening when my father was at home and they'd sit listening to music or watching television together.

She puts the beaker down on the table and clasps her hands tightly again. It looks to me as if she's trying to make herself wait as long as possible before taking another drink. But it's only a few seconds before she releases her tightly interlocking figures, picks up the beaker, drains its contents and goes on with her story.

'Right from the beginning we were comfortably off, much more so than most of our friends. I just thought how clever he must be at his job to be bringing home such a good salary as a young man. But before the end of our first year together, he was bringing home even more money. I tried once or twice to ask him about his work and why he was earning so much, but he never wanted to talk about it. Said it was something I'd never have to worry about as his wife. "You just keep looking nice and taking care of things at home," he'd always tell me before changing the subject. "You won't ever need to get a job. I'll make sure there's always enough money for what we need." He did agree to me working part-time in the boutique after you started school because he knew I was bored and wanted something to fill my time, though he's never been all that keen on the idea. Daddy definitely thinks that a woman's place is in the home.'

She looks at me as if she's hoping that I've heard enough and that she won't have to continue.

'Yes, but I know about all that,' I say. 'I want you to tell me what he's really been doing. And I want you to tell me about the letter and the photos.'

She clasps her hands tighter still. I know that it's not just the effort of telling the truth to *me* that she's finding costly. Having to tell me is probably the first time she's really faced the truth for herself.

'I guess at the back of my mind I've always known that what "the firm" was involved in wasn't completely above board, though it took me a long time to acknowledge that. And even when I did, I rationalised it by telling myself that it must be dealing with the kind of jewellery that's bought by wealthy people with plenty of money to spend and who can afford to pay over the odds. And anyhow, lots of businesses do things that are less than completely honest to avoid paying too much in taxes – that kind of thing...'

Her voice trails away and I guess we're getting closer to the unpalatable truth. The truth from which she's hidden for so long. The truth she's still finding it difficult to acknowledge and even more difficult to put into words. She's biting her lip, something that always annoys her when I do it. And when she notices my surprised expression, she shakes her head and gives an odd-sounding laugh. A laugh in which there is not the merest hint of pleasure or joy.

'Oh, I know – I'm doing what I've told you never to do. I guess I've been more stressed than I realised.' A thick red bubble is forming where she's bitten hard on her lip and blood is beginning to ooze down over her chin. She tears off another piece of kitchen roll and dabs it on her lip to stem the bleeding. 'But I promised you that I'd tell you the truth. So I'd better get on with it…'

Getting on with telling the truth takes the next half hour. First, she stoops down again and reaches into the back of the cupboard from which she'd produced the bottle of wine. This time, however, she brings out half a dozen newspapers, separates them out and spreads them across the table. The one nearest to me carries the banner headline:

BRISTOL JEWELLERS A COVER FOR MASSIVE SMUGGLING ENTERPRISE

The bold, black capitals stretch over the entire front page. Very slowly I read the article underneath. It explains that 'the firm' my father worked for was actually the control centre for a network of criminal gangs engaged in money-laundering and smuggling expensive goods into the country from across the world. The police suspected that it was also linked to gangs importing illegal drugs. But such was the sophistication of the organisation and the level of violence that 'the firm' had previously inflicted on anyone who broke its code of silence that it had been impossible for the authorities to gather sufficient evidence and find the witnesses to bring that part of their investigation to court.

'So Daddy was involved in something really serious,' I say quietly when I've finished reading. 'But *he* wouldn't have done anything cruel to anyone, would he?'

'I hope not,' my mother replies uncertainly as she pushes another newspaper towards me. 'You'd better take a look at this. He might have got an even heavier sentence than five years if he hadn't cooperated with the police.'

I pick up the local paper that she slides across the table and stare at the photo of my father looking as handsome and relaxed as he always did. It's one that was taken professionally two years ago and which my parents included with our family Christmas card. Who among our relatives or friends, I wondered, would have given it to a newspaper reporter? The caption underneath reads simply, 'Bristol businessman Bartholomew Bloom'. The article that accompanies it, however, goes some way to explaining why he spent such long periods away from home.

To neighbours and casual acquaintances in Bristol, Bart Bloom – BB as he was known to many of them – appeared to be nothing more unusual than an obsessive workaholic whose job in the wholesale jewellery trade kept him away from home and family for long periods. The truth was far darker. He was a vital cog in the machinery of an enormous money-laundering and jewellery-smuggling enterprise based in the West Country but with links to organised crime across the UK and on mainland Europe.

Undercover police who tracked his movements over a period of eighteen months discovered he was clocking up almost 90,000 miles a year as he criss-crossed the country in his top-of-the-range Porsche liaising with almost twenty different gangs implicated in what they believe to be one of Britain's biggest and most complex criminal networks.

His role as the smooth-talking 'fixer' at the heart of the operation meant that on his arrest he was uniquely placed to provide details of what was going on and to name those involved. His cooperation in response to the offer of a plea bargain by the Crown Prosecution Service when he was taken into custody has resulted in the ongoing case against nine of the most dangerous and most wanted men in Britain.

His relatively short sentence, given the nature of his offences and the extent of his involvement, reflects the value of the information he has given to the investigation.

But it also makes it highly likely that his life will be in danger from powerful figures in the criminal underworld intent on revenge for what they will undoubtedly see as an act of betrayal. It is assumed that that he will need to enter Witness Protection on his release from prison, something that normally means relocating to another part of the country and changing his identity.

When I glance up from the newspaper, I realise that my mother has been sitting very still and watching me closely. Even the trembling in her hands has stopped. For a moment we look at each other, neither of us, it seems, wanting to put into words what we are thinking. But I know I have to ask my question, even though just forming the words causes a panic to begin to rise in me.

'But does that mean we'll have to move too? That we'll have to leave this house and change our name when Daddy comes out of prison? That'll mean even more pretending. And I don't want to move from here.'

'Well, things are not going to be as simple as you might have thought they would be when you told me it was time for us to stop pretending. I don't think it's going to be possible for us to go on living here in this house.'

I know from the slow, deliberate way she says those words that there's still more unpleasant truth to come.

'I'm afraid there's been a lot of pretending going on,' she adds ominously, 'especially by Daddy.'

'But at least we know now why he spent so much time away from us, don't we?' I ask, seeking some kind of reassurance.

'Oh yes, we do. Or at least I do,' she replies with a long sigh. 'And it wasn't just his work for "the firm". I'm still learning how much pretending Daddy has been doing…'

She stands up slowly and walks a little hesitatingly over to the window, where she steadies herself by leaning on the sink.

'This isn't easy for me to talk about. So it's better if I tell you about it while I'm doing something useful.'

She turns on the tap to fill the sink with water and reaches for some cooking utensils that are piled up ready to be washed by hand.

'The thing is…' She pauses and for a moment I wonder if she's not going to be able to complete her sentence. 'The thing is… that Daddy hasn't been a faithful husband. I had a good idea that something was going on even before the letter and the photos that you saw. In fact, I think I've really known from a few months after we got married, but I've just kept trying to shut it out of my mind. I tried to dismiss it as just an occasional fling. Told myself that that's what men were like. The truth is that it's been a whole lot more complicated than I imagined.'

In the few minutes it takes her to tell me of my father's bizarre lifestyle over more than a decade, she never once turns and looks at me and I never once interrupt her or ask a single question. It's as much as a thirty-three-year-old woman can do just to articulate the words and as much as her thirteen-year-old daughter can cope with just to listen to the information those words convey. The discovery of my father's criminal activities was difficult enough for me to deal with. What I'm about to hear is beyond my comprehension. My first thought is that it will be the story of a man who's been involved in a string of casual affairs with women he's met on his travels. A series of what I've heard described as 'one-night stands'. I'm old enough to know that kind of thing isn't uncommon. But what I actually hear is harder than that to listen to and harder still to understand.

'I don't know the right word for what your father's been doing. He didn't actually *marry* anyone else. So strictly speaking, he's not a bigamist. But he's got another two…' She hesitates as if searching for a more appropriate way to express what she needs to say, '… another two families, if that's the right thing to call them. Another two families in different parts of the country. Another two families just like us – each one with himself and a woman around my age and one child. Another two families that he's treated like he's treated us. Providing for them; giving them the impression that they were the only people he loved; turning up and spending time with them; and then disappearing again. At least, I know about two. Though, goodness knows, he's told me so many lies nothing would surprise me any longer. It seems that the only way in which we've been different from the others is that he did actually *marry* me and he's always come home to us for Christmas and special occasions, even if it's usually been a fleeting visit. I don't know whether I should be grateful for that or if it just makes me even more angry. And I can't even begin to imagine what fantastic excuses he made to the others for the fact that he was never around on high days and holidays.'

She goes on to explain that the police discovered all this when they were gathering evidence and that their investigations had been complicated by the fact that he used a different name with each family. For the first few weeks of their enquiries, they thought they must be dealing with two or three different men rather than just one individual. He was so adept at juggling these assumed identities that even other members of 'the firm' had no idea of his relationships with these women or that he had fathered a child with each of them.

'Well, at least,' she concludes with a hollow laugh, 'with all the practice he's had, he shouldn't find it too difficult to take on a new identity when he gets out of prison.'

There are so many questions racing through my mind. Does she know the names of these other 'families'? What's going to happen to us? Will we have to change our name and move to a different town? Will we have enough money to live on? Will I have to change schools? Will we ever see my father again? The questions go on and on. But before I can work out where to start, the doorbell rings. Uncle Rob and Auntie Cheryl have arrived a little earlier than planned. I'm despatched to let them in and show them to their room while my mother goes upstairs, changes her clothes and reapplies her make-up. Half an hour later, we sit down to supper, all four of us trying to behave as if everything is normal.

I go to my bedroom just after ten o'clock, leaving the three adults talking downstairs. As I close the door behind me to shut out the sound of their voices, I think of the words I'd spoken so adamantly to my mother earlier in the day: *There's a time to stop pretending...* But now that confidence has deserted me. The truth I'd demanded to hear is too much for me. The man I've idolised throughout my childhood is not what I've assumed him to be. Yes, I guessed that I'd be confronted with his shortcomings and I'd prepared myself for that. But what I've heard goes much further than a list of his faults and failings. *His entire life has been a lie.* The past – his past, our family's past, my past – isn't what I thought it was. And now I'm facing a future that frightens me. This isn't what I expected the truth to feel like.

I'm trapped with nowhere to go and no one to turn to. There's no going back to being the child walking along the garden wall and talking to the little lost girl with the blonde curls crying for her parents in Kendrew's Department Store. In fact, I haven't talked to my imaginary friend more than half a dozen times in the past two years and not at all since my thirteenth birthday. Teenagers don't do that kind of thing, I've told myself.

But now *I* am the lost girl. I'm the one who's lost in an adult world that I can't understand and for which I feel totally unprepared. I'm the one who's crying. I'm crying for a father who's become increasingly distant, who's never been what I believed him to be and who is now locked up in jail. And I'm crying for a mother who is locked in a marriage that has never been what she thought it was. A mother who, I'm beginning to learn, is no more equipped to cope with the truth than I am.

I lie on my bed, pull my knees up to my chin and try to put my thoughts in order as I rock backwards and forwards in time to the ticking of the old clock on the wall above the fireplace. I can't bottle all this up inside me. I need to tell someone what's happening. But it's too dark outside for me to walk along the garden wall and talk with someone who isn't really there. And anyway, I've already decided that I'm too grown up for that. I keep rocking backwards and forwards and slowly an idea begins to form itself in my mind. I know what I can do... I can put it all down on paper. Better still, I can write it in a letter. That'll be just like writing to a penfriend, won't it?

I stop rocking and sit on the edge of the bed for a couple of minutes to gather my thoughts. There's an old half-filled exercise book in which I sometimes scribble things I have to do. I open it at a blank page, take a pencil out of the pen pot, sharpen it carefully, and begin to write...

Dear Calippa...

It's half past eleven when I put the pencil down and close the exercise book. Nothing has changed. My father is in prison, my mother is taking refuge in obsessive activity and excessive drinking, and we will almost certainly have to leave the house I love. But things are a little easier just for having written down what has happened and how I'm feeling. I have no idea what the future will bring. Nor do I realise that this will be the first of hundreds of letters that I will write to my unseen penfriend over the years in what will become a substantial pile of exercise books. None of those letters will ever be removed from the book, folded up and slipped into an envelope. But they will become a commentary to my life that will help me through some of its most difficult moments and provide me with a record without which it will be impossible to tell the rest of my story.

And they keep the memory alive in me of that little girl with the curly blonde hair lost and alone in Kendrew's Department Store. I think I understand her feelings better tonight than ever before.

4
Christmas Eve 1988
Lori Bloom, you've really
changed...

Christmas Eve at Cumberland Cottage feels quite different from those I've spent at our house in Morley Road on the outskirts of Bristol. One of only seven dwellings in the picture postcard hamlet of Riventhwaite, the cottage sits by itself at the end of a narrow track almost hidden from the main road overlooking Wythmere, one of the Lake District's smaller and lesser-known but no less beautiful stretches of water.

It's a larger and grander property than its unpretentious name would suggest. What had been three humble labourers' cottages when they were built in the eighteenth century were converted, with the addition of a generous extension for the kitchen and dining area, into one spacious family home in the 1970s. Uncle Rob and Auntie Cheryl bought the property a decade later and, as they never tire of reciting to their guests, have spent a lot of money in 'painstakingly restoring many of its original features while ensuring that the modern conveniences and gadgets with which we've filled it merge unobtrusively and tastefully with its olde-worlde charm'.

The guests on this occasion listening to the oft-repeated narrative are the Hodgsons, a family whose roots in that part of the country reach back to the 1800s, and my mother and me. They've been invited because Roger Hodgson is Uncle Rob's partner in an investment firm they set up some years ago and he and his wife, Eleanor, have formed a friendship with my uncle and aunt that goes beyond their business relationship. My mother and I arrived earlier today and we'll be staying until New Year because our house has been sold and we're now living in a small two-bedroom flat less than a mile away from Morley Road.

'You don't have room to put us up,' Uncle Rob insisted over the phone to my mother at the beginning of December. 'So you must come to us this Christmas. Let's make it the start of a new family tradition. And anyhow it'll be good for you to be looked after. You've been through more than enough these past couple of years.'

He's right about it being good for her to be looked after. She found my father's arrest and imprisonment difficult to cope with, and the further revelations of his bizarre personal life have taken a heavy toll on her. As the divorce proceedings she set in motion immediately after he was sentenced took their course, her drinking steadily increased until it reached the point where she had to spend three months in a residential rehab programme in the summer of 1987. Fortunately, I remained best friends with Sarah Tattersall from junior school who also goes to George Fulford College. A little pressure from her was enough to persuade her parents to take me in during that time.

My mother came back home just as the divorce was being finalised. After all the legal wranglings were complete there was considerably less money than she'd anticipated and the house I loved so much had to be put on the market. But there were just sufficient funds, with a little financial help from Uncle Rob, for her to put a deposit on the flat and to cover my fees at George Fulford College, provided she increased the hours she worked at the boutique.

I've made up my mind that I never want to see my father again. But I miss him terribly, even though his visits home were infrequent. In the two years prior to his arrest, I saw him on no more than a dozen occasions, and then usually only for two or three days at a time. Yet somehow, despite his long absences, and in a way that's hard to understand looking back, he remained a constant presence in my childhood.

And now there are moments when a fierce anger at what he's done and a bitter resentment at how life has turned out for us as a result of his actions will suddenly flood over me. I've learned to deal with those times by burying my feelings as deep as I can and throwing myself into my schoolwork. But they're at their worst when I'm at my most emotionally and physically vulnerable. Those low points come with a sickening regularity and predictability that I can literally mark on the calendar. My mother dismisses my efforts to explain how much pain I'm in and how awful I feel by telling me that every woman has occasional bad periods, that I just have to learn to deal with it, and that it will get easier as I get older. But it never does get any easier, and for a week in every month I feel as if I'm walking through a thick fog with a heavy weight in my stomach that makes every movement an effort.

But just yesterday I emerged out of one of those dark periods with the familiar surge of relief that always comes when I realise that it's over for another month. And today my mood lifts even more when the car pulls up at the end of the gravel track that leads to Cumberland Cottage.

Uncle Rob, who loves every opportunity to play the role of host, is waiting for us. As he steps out of the doorway and comes towards the car, I can see the lavishly decorated Douglas fir tree standing in the hallway and what looks like a small mountain of gifts arranged carefully underneath.

'Angela, it's good to see you looking so much more like yourself,' he says as he lifts our suitcases out of the boot, sets them on the ground and hugs my mother. 'And the Lake District air will do you the world of good.'

He's about to pick the suitcases up again when he stops and turns to me.

'No, it can't be,' he exclaims with the exaggerated voice of a Shakespearean actor and a look of mock surprise. 'But it really is you, isn't it? Goodness me, Lori Bloom, you've really changed. You've grown into such a fine young woman. Whatever happened to that little girl we used to spend Christmas with in Bristol?'

He leads us into the house and Auntie Cheryl comes hurrying from the kitchen to greet us. While she and my mother embrace each other, Uncle Rob beckons to me to follow him up the old oak-wood staircase of which he's so proud and on which he's spent so much money and effort to restore to its original condition.

Instead of going left at the top of the stairs to the small bedroom where I usually sleep when we visit them, he turns right and shows me into the large room that overlooks Wythmere.

'We've given your mum the other bedroom with the view of the lake,' he says as he sets my suitcase on the bed. 'But I thought it was time that you had something better than the smallest bedroom tucked away at the back of the house. A young lady like you needs a room with an en suite bathroom and a full-length mirror so she can make sure she looks just right before she makes her appearance with the other guests. Does this suit you alright?'

I throw my arms round him, kiss him on the cheek and assure him that it suits me just fine.

'Well, you enjoy it,' he responds, stroking my hair. 'After all, you're my favourite niece. So nothing but the best for you. The Hodgsons will be here for lunch in just under an hour. I think you'll like their son, Reuben. He's a good-looking boy. A year or so older than you, I think. Very popular with the girls, I hear. But he seemed particularly interested when I showed him a photo of you and told him you'd be here for Christmas. So you might want to make a good impression when you come down.'

He gives me a knowing wink and a quick peck on the cheek before he leaves me to sort my things out and get ready.

As soon as the door clicks shut behind him, I unpack my case, hang my clothes up in the wardrobe and turn my attention to what I should wear for lunch. If Reuben

Hodgson is half as interesting as Uncle Rob has made him sound, it'll be worth making an effort. And it's an opportunity to make a fashion statement by wearing the outfit I've been assembling and trying on for the past month.

I get changed and take a long look in the full-length mirror. I like what I see. The soft cotton, loose-fitting, navy-blue shorts with their all-over half-moon pattern show off my long, slim legs to their best advantage. The beige cord jacket – from which I've cut off the arms with pinking shears for just the right laid-back effect – sits perfectly over the neon-yellow, skin-tight, ribbed Lycra tank top that makes me feel very sexy. The string of plain wooden beads round my neck that I found only after hours of searching through second-hand shops is the perfect accessory. And one glance at my feet confirms for me that the plain white leather trainers I'm wearing complete the relaxed teenage look I've been aiming to achieve.

When I showed it to my mother she was a little less impressed than I'd anticipated and suggested that it was 'just a little too summery' for this time of year. But I put her negative opinion down to her age and decided to ignore her criticism.

Uncle Rob is right. I *have* changed. And I can't help but feel pleased and surprised at how I've altered since last Christmas. For the first ten years of my life I had absolutely no interest in clothes. I had a little round tummy which meant that every attempt my mother made to dress me in a skirt was doomed to failure. Either it had to be pulled over the inconvenient bulge, giving the impression that the waistband was sitting just under my armpits. Or it slipped under my little pot belly so that it was in constant danger of falling down completely. I was certainly not the sweet little girl my mother had hoped I'd be.

Looking back, I have an image of myself as a child, permanently dressed in a bluish-grey tracksuit with what were then called 'pixie boots' on my feet. I guess I must have looked a particularly plump and ungraceful pixie. Reaching the age of twelve and getting into my early teens coincided with me discovering that I was short-sighted and needed to wear glasses, which only added to my generally nerdy appearance and my growing reputation as the school swot. Of course, I must have worn other clothes at home and at weekends, but in my memories of those years I'm always wearing school uniform.

But something quite unexpected happened around the time of my fourteenth birthday. My friendship with Sarah Tattersall had flourished as we helped each other make the adjustment to a very different school environment from what we'd known at Corton Primary, and she was the one who first made me aware of the change to which I'd been oblivious. One of the boys had gone out of his way to sit near us in a science lesson and I nudged her to tell her that he was looking at her.

'You really don't know, do you?' she said with an incredulous expression on her face. 'It's you he's looking at, Lori. You've really changed in this last little while. You've kind of grown up – all of a sudden. You've always been the cleverest girl in our year, but now we all think you're the most attractive as well. The boys certainly think that too. I've heard them talking about you.'

My initial response was that she was having fun at my expense or just trying to make me feel better about myself. But she was serious. She was neither joking nor flattering me. And as the months passed and the interest of the boys became increasingly obvious, I began to enjoy my new-found celebrity as the most desirable girl in our form. My confidence had taken a hard knock after my father's trial and conviction, but this level of attention gave me a new self-assurance. I could see whenever I got out of the shower or when I stopped to look at myself in the mirror that I really had changed. I was no longer an awkward little girl and my funny little tummy had gone. Nor was I the gawky thirteen-year-old who always felt slightly out of place. Without at first being aware of it, I was becoming a young woman. I'd inherited my mother's shapely figure and something of my father's good looks and his thick black hair. And I liked how I felt and looked. If the thoroughly unpleasant week I had to go through every month was the price I had to pay for who I was becoming, then it might even be worth all that it cost me.

But there was something else I quickly came to enjoy even more than just how I looked. My mother's dire warnings about the dangers of 'getting carried away' and finding myself pregnant had combined with a general distrust of men that arose from my father's infidelity and dishonesty. It was a merging of exhortation and experience that made me wary of ever losing control of myself in any relationship with a member of the opposite sex. I began to realise that I never needed to be at the mercy of any man. I was the one who was attractive and desirable. So I could be the one who made the rules. I could be the one who held the power. I could be the one who played with the affections of someone else. And very quickly, what had begun as a proper desire to protect myself against being hurt developed into an ability to manipulate the affections and actions of people who were drawn to me. I'd seen it work to surprising effect with two or three of the boys at school whom I'd played off against each other.

And as I turn away from the mirror and get ready to join the others for lunch, I can think of no reason why it shouldn't work now. After the build-up that Uncle Rob has given him, I really want to see how Reuben Hodgson will react to Lori Bloom.

I stay in my room until I hear the Hodgsons arrive and then wait another ten minutes until I'm sure they'll be settled and having drinks in the lounge. At last, *it's time to make my entry*. I've heard Uncle Rob tell the story more than once of how his obsessive attention to detail included instructing the contractors who carried out the renovations not to eliminate the creakiness in the stairs. 'We don't want to lose the authentic feel of the old house,' he'd told the somewhat bemused foreman. And since that creaky stairway ends by the open door that leads from the hallway to the lounge, every step I take will be an opportunity to announce my imminent arrival.

It's a strategy that works perfectly. As I approach the bottom step I hear Uncle Rob's voice.

'Ah, that must be her coming down the stairs.'

I can see through the open door that he's stood up and he's walking across the room to welcome me and introduce me to his guests. There's a fleeting look of surprise on his face when he sees me, and he seems to hesitate for a moment as I step confidently into the room. But he quickly regains his composure and takes me by the hand.

'Mr and Mrs Hodgson, meet my niece, Lori Bloom.'

As he speaks his face loses its initial expression of disbelief and assumes a look that's a mixture of sympathetic reassurance to me and an unspoken plea to his guests to be understanding of my youthful lack of awareness of what was suitable attire for such an occasion. And as the Hodgsons get up to greet me I realise with a sinking feeling just how ridiculously out of place my clothes are. They're dressed in well-tailored tweeds, expensive woollens and the kind of brown leather brogues beloved of country gentry. And their choice of apparel has clearly been anticipated and copied by everyone else in the room. It isn't just Uncle Rob and Auntie Cheryl and my mother who've taken their cue from the Hodgsons. More to the point, their son Reuben, whom I've been hoping to impress, is wearing jeans and a sweater. But they're entirely appropriate for his age. They're well chosen and good quality, and they fit with what everyone else in the room – apart from me – is wearing.

I stand stock still, unable to move or make a sound, like a startled deer that's been caught in the headlights of the Hodgson's Range Rover on a lakeside road at night. My face is flushed with embarrassment and my eyes are stinging as I try in vain to fight back the tears. I've never felt so stupid or out of place in my life. I'm vaguely aware of my mother looking at me and slowly shaking her head as Mrs Hodgson reaches out to shake my hand and says very politely that it's nice to meet me. Her husband is smiling as he takes a step forward and gently eases his wife aside.

'Well, Lori,' he says, looking straight into my eyes in a way that tells me he knows exactly how I'm feeling. 'I'm going to give you a hug, if you don't mind. You're making me wish I was young again. Look at us, stuffy bunch that we are, perspiring in our winter clothes in a delightfully cosy room. Seems to me that you're the only one young enough and brave enough to dress in exactly the right way for a Christmas Eve lunch.'

He turns to his son, who's been standing back watching what's been happening with his hands in his pockets and a broad grin on his face.

'Remember your manners, Reuben, and get yourself over here. Let me apologise for my son,' he says, resuming his smile and focusing his attention on me once again. 'You know, Lori, sometimes I wonder if that boy's learned anything I've tried to teach him. When I was his age, I wouldn't have needed anybody to tell me what to do when a young lady like you walked into the room. I'd have been first in the queue to doff my cap and tell her that I was at her service.'

Reuben, who'd obviously imbibed his father's talent for handling awkward situations and putting people at their ease, saluted smartly, clicked his heels and gave a quick *yessir* before walking across the room to me. Unlike his parents, he didn't shake my hand or hug me. He just slipped his hands back into his pockets and grinned again.

'Hi Lori. Your uncle's been telling us all about you. I thought he was probably exaggerating. But now that I've seen you, I'm thinking he was telling the truth. You really are as different as he said. And I'm really pleased you're here. I was worried that I'd be stuck with all these stuffy middle-aged people on my own. We can sit next to each other at lunch and talk about something interesting.'

I'm still struggling to work out exactly what's happened in the last five minutes and completely unable to find the right words to respond. Uncle Rob comes to my rescue as he summons everyone to lunch.

'Well, that's just what I hoped you two youngsters would do – be company for each other. And Cheryl's just about to serve up. So come on through to the dining room and let's eat.'

Auntie Cheryl is an even better cook than my mother – a family skill, alas, that has not been passed on to me. I know it must be an excellent meal. But, delicious as it is, my mind is definitely not on the food No one comments on my lack of appetite, so I must appear to be tucking in as heartily as anyone else, particularly since I haven't eaten any breakfast since we left Bristol earlier this morning. But there is so much going on around me and my thoughts are racing so quickly that there simply isn't room in my head to think about what we're eating. I can't quite believe that what was such an excruciatingly embarrassing situation when I stepped into the lounge a few minutes ago has been completely transformed by the time we sit down to lunch. I expected to be the butt of derision, or at best the object of pity. But now I find myself the centre of attention as the Hodgsons ask me about my education and my hopes for the future and even quiz me on my fashion sense. Now that everyone has got over the initial shock of my appearance it's become a topic for conversation.

But what occupies my mind more than anything else is the presence of the boy sitting to my right. I'm quickly learning that he is every bit as interesting as Uncle Rob has made him sound. Since I've been old enough to think about such things, my template for what makes a man attractive has been my father with his smoothed-back jet-black hair and his obvious good looks. Reuben Hodgson is nothing like that. His hair is what's often disparagingly referred to as mousy-brown, though for some reason it makes me think of the colour of bark on a weathered old tree. And it seems to have a life of its own, an uncompromising independence that makes it stubbornly resistant to any attempts to force it into submission by a comb or hairbrush.

Unlike my father, no one would ever think of comparing him to a Hollywood matinee idol. His face, still retaining signs of his childhood freckles, is too broad to be described as handsome in any normal sense. But it has the almost permanent expression of someone who finds life interesting and amusing. I noticed his grin the moment I walked into the lounge. And now I can see that it disappears, or rather changes, only when it morphs into a laugh, something that happens frequently. But his sense of humour isn't of the kind that manifests itself in telling carefully rehearsed jokes or relating funny stories of past events. It's much more centred in the moment – constantly spotting the little incongruities of life, celebrating the ridiculous and offering a running commentary on whatever is happening. And before we're halfway through lunch, I know that this is not a boy I could bend to my will like the boys in my class at school. And I'm desperately hoping that he likes me.

Whether it's simply the pleasure of the company we're sharing and the meal we've just eaten or the initial impact of my inappropriate dress sense and the response it has provoked, I don't know. But their visit is going so well that the Hodgsons readily agree to Uncle Rob's suggestion that they should stay on into the afternoon and early evening.

As so often happens in this part of the country, the misty drizzle of the morning has given way to broken cloud, and the general consensus is that we should take advantage of the improvement in the weather. A walk by the side of the lake will be just the right thing after such an enjoyable lunch. I can see immediately that this is a proposal that offers a perfect opportunity to get to know Reuben Hodgson a little better, and I rush upstairs to change into more suitable clothing. I'm grateful that, despite my reluctance to agree, my mother insisted on me bringing some more suitable outdoor clothing and walking shoes.

The seven of us – the three Hodgsons, Uncle Rob and Auntie Cheryl, and my mother and me – set off together and I begin to wonder if my hopes are about to be dashed. Everyone strolling along in a group isn't what I had envisaged. To my relief, however, when we reach the edge of the lake the path quickly narrows, allowing space for only two people to walk side by side. Trying not to make my intentions too obvious, I step aside to let the adults go first and fall into step with Reuben at the rear of the procession. The further we walk around the lake, the more the distance between the two of us and the others increases. This is exactly what I've been hoping for. Now I have him all to myself!

I can remember just about every moment of that walk. The weather is mild and the clouds part to allow the sun to break through, giving everything that quality of light and shade that you find only in places where hills and deep water are so close that they complement each other as perfectly as in a landscape painting by a great master. The view to the snow-capped mountains in the distance is awe-inspiring, reminding me of a scene from *The Lord of the Rings*, the book I've been reading for the last few weeks. The breeze that whips across the lake from time to time is enough to ruffle our hair and make us laugh at each other as it forces us to catch our breath. And the most vivid memories of all are the words and phrases, even whole sentences, that I can still recall and recite to myself from our conversation. It's a conversation stilted at first by my shyness in the presence of a boy quite unlike any other I've ever encountered. But it's soon eased and liberated by his irrepressible sense of fun and his easy confidence in the presence of a girl he's helped to rescue from an embarrassing situation earlier in the day.

I don't fully appreciate it now, but I will frequently look back on that afternoon as a rare moment of innocence in a world from which simple goodness is so often conspicuously absent. When I left Bristol this morning, my understanding of relationships between men and women was dominated by the painful experience of my father's betrayal and by my resolute determination to be on my guard against ever becoming the victim of the kind of treachery to which my mother was subjected. Now I'm walking on a lakeside path, talking and laughing with a boy I met only a few hours ago and wishing for the first time in my life that time would stand still. It even flashes through my mind that as soon as I get back home I'll make my mother happy by getting rid of the old station waiting room clock that I insisted on taking with us when we moved house... a thought I will dismiss after a few moments' reflection the next day, however. We are two naïve young people, barely more than children, and for that brief moment we have not a care in the world nor any concern for what the future might bring.

We reach the end of Wythmere where the path begins to climb away from the water's edge before descending to a little sandy beach and then leads back home on the other side of the lake. The adults are two or three hundred yards ahead of us, momentarily out of sight, and Reuben suggests that we sit down on the bench that's been strategically placed there to give ramblers the opportunity to rest and look up the full length of the lake.

'They'll be too busy talking to miss us for a bit.' He pauses and grins at me, before saying slowly and quietly, 'I think I'd like to enjoy the view properly for a few minutes.'

I suspect that his thoughts aren't entirely focused on the glittering water of the lake that stretches ahead of us. But he is either too gentlemanly or too experienced in this kind of thing to rush matters. We sit side by side for almost a minute without saying anything else. I can feel my heart beating and I'm not sure what to do next. He just sits there, taking deep breaths and gazing straight ahead. Then he slips his hand into mine and turns slowly to face me.

'You know,' he says, his grin wider than ever, 'one day I'm going to swim in this lake. But right now, I think you're a lot nicer to look at than the lake. And, if you don't mind, I'm going to kiss you.'

The kiss is as different from the snogging that happens at school dances and the like as glorious sunshine is from the flickering light of a candle on a windy night. It is my first proper kiss. The first time I've longed to be kissed. The first time I've wanted a kiss to last forever. I'm not entirely sure what is the appropriate thing to do when our lips part. But I mutter something about it being nice and add an embarrassed 'thank you'. That's enough to set Reuben laughing again.

'You're funny. And you're the first girl who's ever thanked me for kissing her. I like that.' He takes hold of my hand again and pulls me up from the bench. 'Come on. We'd better catch up to the others before they start asking what we've been up to.'

After we get back to Cumberland Cottage, the Hodgsons are easily dissuaded from getting into their car, and sandwiches and drinks are quickly prepared just in case our walk has left us in need of yet more food. Then we sit around the log fire in the lounge, playing games and chatting about everything and anything until almost half past eight. And before they leave, we stand in a circle, hold hands and sing along together to Cliff Richard's 'Mistletoe and Wine'. It occurs to me that I've never known a Christmas song with lyrics more appropriate to what we're actually doing and how I'm feeling. There are logs on *our* fire and gifts on *our* tree. And I'm certainly rejoicing in all the good things of the day. I glance at Reuben, who's positioned himself next to me so that he can hold my hand, and it really does feel as if the past has gone and this is a new beginning.

It's almost ten o'clock by the time I say goodnight to my mother, Uncle Rob and Auntie Cheryl and climb the creaky stairs. I close the bedroom door quietly behind me, switch on the bedside light and walk across to the window, where I stand looking out for a full five minutes before I draw the curtains. I can see the water at the edge of the lake glistening with the reflection of the light from the downstairs windows. It's too dark to make out the path where we walked earlier. But in my imagination I retrace our footsteps that afternoon, replay our conversation and remember the kiss on the bench at the end of the lake.

It's been a long day and I'm tired. I brush my teeth and get ready for bed. But there's still one more thing I have to do. I unzip the compartment on the front of my case and pull out the blue exercise book that I picked out from the small pile under my bed at home and brought with me. I've already filled ten of them with letters I've written to Calippa Cumberland every night since Christmas Eve two years ago. There are only a few pages left in this one. Just enough to take me to the end of the year. Sometimes I fill whole pages with reflections on the day that's gone. But tonight, there's only one thing I need to record:

Dear Calippa

I think I've fallen in love! It's a strange feeling and I don't know if I'll be able to sleep tonight. In some ways it's like being found by the person I've been waiting for all my life. Or maybe I feel more lost than ever. But lost in an exciting new way, lost in a world where all kinds of surprising things will happen and where I hope I'll eventually learn to find my way around. Who knows?

I need to sleep now.

Goodnight.

Your friend, Lori

5
Christmas Eve 1992
There's no time like the present...

The new family tradition that Uncle Rob proposed just four years ago is already firmly established. This is the fourth year that my mother and I have travelled from Bristol to spend Christmas with him and Auntie Cheryl in Riventhwaite. And the visit of the Hodgsons on Christmas Eve in time for lunch before we all take a leisurely stroll round Wythmere has already become an essential part of a seasonal ritual that we have all assumed will continue long into the future. But today the familiar routine we've been so eagerly anticipating until just a few weeks ago has been significantly altered. Instead of meeting up at Cumberland Cottage just before noon, we've joined the Hodgsons some fifteen miles away at ten o'clock this morning to collect an object that will allow us to complete a very different ritual, one that's in stark contrast to our customary celebrations. And when we all arrive back at the cottage at half past twelve, one member of our usual company is missing.

We get out of the two cars in which we've travelled and file into the house – Uncle Rob and Auntie Cheryl followed by Mr and Mrs Hodgson, with my mother and me coming on behind. We take off our warm coats and sit down to lunch. But we have little appetite for the food that's been set out. It's a while before anyone speaks. Conversation is something for which none of us can summon up sufficient will or find adequate words. It's as much as we can do to begin to come to grips with the truth we will never be able to escape. This is not a bad dream from which we will wake tomorrow morning. It's a terrible reality with which we will have to live for the rest of our days. A reality that broke in on us just six weeks ago. A reality that has destroyed the dreams and hopes that have filled my thoughts for the last four years.

My feelings for Reuben Hodgson proved to be more than a passing phase. My mother, concerned as always that I shouldn't get hurt in a relationship with a boy, warned me that those feelings could and probably would suddenly change. That, she never tired of telling me, was just an inevitable part of growing up. But, far from dissipating or even disappearing altogether, my love for Reuben actually grew stronger with the passing of time. And just as important, Reuben felt exactly the same way about me.

Looking back with the experience – or maybe the weary cynicism – of the years, I can see how unlikely it might have seemed to the adults around us that a teenage crush that began with a kiss on a lakeside bench would flourish into something deep and lasting. But that's exactly what happened. And by the summer of 1992 we were planning to get married when I'd graduated from university and he'd completed his studies at agricultural college in Cumbria.

Riventhwaite is much closer than Bristol to St Andrews, where I'm studying for my degree. And in addition, Uncle Rob has taken on the role that my father never really played even before my parents' divorce. This means that Cumberland Cottage in effect has become a home from home, the place where I spend most of my time when not at university. I've even brought my much-loved station waiting room clock from Bristol and hung it above my bed, where I can hear its comforting tick whenever I wake.

The move had the added benefit of enabling me to see much more of Reuben than would otherwise have been the case and allowing our relationship to continue to develop.

Everyone who knew us agreed that we complemented each other perfectly – my predisposition to lose myself in a world of books and study was balanced by his irrepressible sense of humour, his love for the outdoor life and his pleasure in anything that involved growing things and getting his hands dirty in the soil of his native county. All seemed set fair for our future together. But my mother's nagging fears that I would be hurt were to be realised in a way that neither she nor I could ever have imagined.

On a cold morning in the middle of November 1992 Reuben had called at Cumberland Cottage at Uncle Rob's request to offer some advice on how the garden might be extended and adapted to provide more space for planting and growing vegetables in the spring. By the time they'd surveyed the land available and worked out their plans, both of them were pretty well wet through. They'd been too engrossed in their conversation to stop even for a moment and fetch a couple of umbrellas when a sudden rainstorm had blown in across the lake. Uncle Rob suggested that before he drove off, Reuben should come into the cottage to have a quick shower and a hot drink while his clothes dried off on a radiator. Reuben readily agreed but, on a sudden whim, decided that since he was already soaked to the skin, he'd go for broke and have a swim before accepting the invitation.

'The first time I kissed Lori,' he explained, grinning as he stripped off his clothes, 'I told her I was going to swim in Wythmere one day. But I've never actually done it and I don't want her to think she's going to marry a man who doesn't mean what he says. There's no time like the present. So you can be the witness that I've kept my word. And I'll appreciate the warm shower all the more.'

He ran down to the water's edge and splashed into the lake while Uncle Rob looked on, shaking his head good-naturedly at what he considered such youthful bravado.

'It's cold but it feels good,' Reuben called out, turning around to face the shore and waving. 'I think it's what you call "bracing". Anyhow, I'm gonna swim to the other side and back. I should do that easily in twenty minutes. I'll want that hot drink when I'm done.'

Cumberland Cottage stands near the head of Wythmere where the lake is no more than a quarter of a mile wide, a favourite spot for freshwater swimmers. Uncle Rob stood and watched Reuben's progress for five minutes before he went back into the kitchen. Reuben's estimate of the time it should take was just about right, he reckoned, as he draped a towel over the radiator to warm, and chuckled to himself at the thought of his visitor coming through the door, shivering and dripping all over the kitchen floor.

He glanced out of the window and thought he could make out a lone figure swimming back from the far shore. It was time to put the kettle on. When it came to the boil, he looked out again just to reassure himself that all was well. This time, however, he could see nothing but the unbroken surface of the lake mirroring the slate-grey colour of the cloud-covered sky. Nothing to worry about, he told himself. Reuben was probably scrambling onto the shore a couple of hundred yards further down the lake.

All the same, probably best to go outside and take a better look. But there was no sign of the returning swimmer. He half-walked, half-ran to the lakeside, straining his eyes to scan across the water. Still he could see nothing. He called out Reuben's name several times but there was no reply. Now he was worried, beginning to panic, even. For a moment or two he stood still, took slow breaths, and tried to tell himself that everything was alright, that he was fretting needlessly, that any minute he'd hear a familiar voice and Reuben would emerge from the water laughing at his concerned expression. But there was no sound and no sign of the young man he was looking for. He turned around, ran back to Cumberland Cottage and dialled 999.

Two police frogmen found Reuben's body late the following afternoon, just as the light was beginning to fade and they were about to call off the search for the day. His parents and my uncle and aunt watched from the kitchen window as they brought his body back to the shore and laid it gently on the spot from which he'd set out on his ill-fated swim a little more than twenty-four hours earlier.

After having rushed from my student lodgings at the University of St Andrews the previous evening and been awake all night and all through the morning, I was asleep in the large upstairs bedroom. Ever since I'd first slept there four Christmases before, Uncle Rob had decreed it to be my room whenever we visited Riventhwaite, and I retreated there just before noon, utterly exhausted and unable to keep my eyes open any longer.

They roused me from sleep and helped me downstairs and into the lounge to break the news to me that his body had been found. I insisted on being taken to the door of the cottage just as the lifeless body of the twenty-one-year-old man I loved and had hoped to marry was being lifted into the waiting vehicle. I remember hearing a long and uncanny howl of utter despair. It was like the cry of a wounded animal caught in some cruel trap, and I wondered where such a hideous noise could be coming from. I desperately wanted someone to make it stop, until I was struck with the dreadful realisation that it was coming from deep within me. Then I felt myself crumpling into Uncle Rob's arms and sobbing hysterically.

The weeks that followed that terrible moment merge into what I recall as a dismal, strength-sapping, pointless journey through the longest and blackest of tunnels in which I stumbled and collapsed repeatedly as the constantly shifting ground gave way beneath my feet. The darkness clung to me like a thick and heavy blanket, weighing me down so that even the simplest task or the most basic thought demanded an effort of will of which I was utterly incapable.

I have vague and confused memories of well-intentioned voices sympathising with my loss, telling me not to give up, encouraging me to keep going, promising me that a new day would dawn, assuring me that life would be worth living again. But they were hollow words and empty platitudes that served only to push me deeper into darkness and despair.

I remember, as if it were a dream, a sympathetic doctor visiting and prescribing some kind of medication that he said 'will help you over the crisis'. It probably enabled me to function at some level but it did nothing to ease the grief and pain that gripped me like an ever-tightening vice.

I was still in a state of shock nearly three weeks later when I attended the inquest, where the coroner recorded a verdict of death by misadventure. The post-mortem had been inconclusive but the doctor who carried out the examination of the body was of the opinion that, rather than being the result of drowning, Reuben's death had been caused by cardiac arrest. He put this down to what he called *ventricular fibrillation*, a kind of abnormal heart rhythm that can occur in otherwise healthy young men and which, in rare cases, can even cause the heart to stop beating completely. He was unable to give a reason for why this had happened other than that it could have been triggered by a combination of unusual exertion and the coldness of the water. The coroner said some sympathetic words to those of us sat in the court, urged people to be careful when swimming in open water, and delivered his verdict of death by misadventure.

I have hated that word *misadventure* ever since that day. It takes the word *adventure* – a word I loved as a child, a word that encapsulated everything to which I looked forward, a word full of excitement and anticipation – and with the addition of those three letters turns it into a word filled with a terrible dread of the mistakes and mishaps and misfortunes that await us at every turn.

And now on this Christmas Eve, when church bells will be rung and carols sung throughout the land, when children will be going to bed scarcely able to sleep with excitement at what the morning will bring, when parents will be secretively wrapping presents and perpetuating the myth of an ancient saint who will once again bring gifts to every home, we are slowly getting up from the table, leaving our half-finished lunch, and setting off reluctantly to tread the same path round Wythmere that we have happily walked together at this same hour of the day for the last four years.

But this time it will not be the usual joyous procession accompanied by the music of laughter and happy conversation. Instead of holding the hand of the boy I love, I will be holding a wooden box containing his ashes. That's another word I've hated since then: *ashes*. The very sound of it, the way it seems to stick to the roof of your mouth, the way you're forced to spit it out to complete the word, fills me with revulsion. It's a horrible but entirely fitting word for the incinerated debris of what was once a living, breathing, loving human being.

Attending the cremation three days ago was a terrible experience: listening to a clergyman who didn't know Reuben spout pious platitudes that none of us believed, and trying to figure out why his parents, who had only tenuous links with the church in their village, thought it was necessary to have a religious service. And the moment that really turned my grief to anger was watching the coffin retreat behind a curtain to the strains of Whitney Houston singing the song that was topping the charts that week, 'I Will Always Love You'. I think I must have been the only person there who realised the hideous irony of playing a song that was part of the soundtrack of a movie called *The Bodyguard*. If only there had been a bodyguard with Reuben when he set out to swim across the lake. If only...

But this is worse. It's meant to be a final dignified goodbye, a celebration of Reuben's life, a tribute to his love of Wythmere and the Lake District. Instead, it feels to me like an act of abject surrender, a simpering acceptance of the truth that the dark and merciless primeval power of the lake has swallowed its latest victim, robbed him of his life and stolen from me the person I loved most in all the world. But what we're about to do is the wish of his parents, and any objection from me would only increase the anguish they feel at the loss of their only child.

We reach the wooden bench on which Reuben happily told me of his intention to swim in the lake one day, the bench on which he and I sat and kissed for the first time. The little bronze panel that was attached to the bench yesterday in preparation for what we are doing now glints in the shaft of sunlight that has unexpectedly broken through the clouds. It has taken us hours of discussion to agree on twenty-four simple words:

In memory of Reuben Hodgson
who shared a first kiss here
who lost his life in this lake
and who will always be loved

No one is quite sure what to say, so we stand in an awkward silence. The only sound is the lapping of the water on the shore a few feet in front of us. I'm struggling to comprehend how something as calm as the untroubled water of the lake appears at this moment could have extinguished the life of a strong and healthy young man.

After a moment or two, Uncle Rob gently takes from me the wooden casket I'm holding. It feels like a stab to my heart when I release my grip and relinquish it into his hands. I'm struck with the sudden realisation that it's all I have left of Reuben, and now I have to let even that go – let it go not just to someone else but to the dark and chilly depths of Wythmere.

It's only as Uncle Rob passes it to Reuben's parents that I notice that the lid has been painted with a woodland scene of bluebells in full bloom. I've been staring straight ahead and my eyes have been so filled with tears as we walked along the lakeside path that I've failed to see clearly what I've been holding in my hands. I'm touched by its exquisite beauty and yet appalled that something so lovely should have been created for such a purpose.

My mother and I stand with my Uncle Rob and Auntie Cheryl, the four of us holding hands. The Hodgsons step forward, kneel together by the water's edge and set the casket on the ground in front of them. Roger Hodgson removes the lid and passes it to his wife. His hands are trembling slightly and he takes a moment to steady them.

Then, very slowly and deliberately, he pours the contents into the lake while the six of us, as we have agreed, repeat in unison, 'Goodbye, Reuben. We will always love you.'

As funeral rites go it is brief and basic. It has neither lofty language nor resonant ritual and it carries no pretence of hope for an afterlife. But it perfectly expresses the sense of hopelessness and loss that binds us together in this moment. And it does succeed in bringing me to the place where I realise that I have no more tears left to cry. There is nothing more to be done.

The Hodgsons get up from the ground, and after a moment's hesitation, we return silently to Cumberland Cottage.

Tonight, long after the Hodgsons have left us and gone home, and long after everyone else in the house is asleep, I sit by the open window looking out into the darkness. I can see nothing of the lake or even of the path we walked on, but I can hear the water, still lapping as gently and persistently as it did this afternoon and as it will do for the rest of time. Everything will go on as it has done since time began. There will still be scenes of beauty, sounds that move us, places that hold special memories. But I have come to a terrible conclusion. Those things can no longer hide the truth that the universe is unaware of our deepest longings and uncaring about our most grievous wounds.

I shiver, but it isn't just the chill night air blowing in through the window that is making me cold. It is the terrible sense of desolation, of being lonely and lost and abandoned. And I realise that this is something I've feared since the day I heard the message of the little lost girl come over the tannoy in Kendrew's Department Store. This, I tell myself sadly, is how it ever was and how it ever will be. It is the bleak truth at the very core of our existence in this world. We can ignore it for a time, we can distract ourselves with work or pleasure. But it is always lying in wait for us, ready to reassert itself whenever our guard is down.

And I know that for me there is only one way to deal with it and retain my sanity. I can write. I can share what I believe to be the terrible truth with someone who will understand.

I take an exercise book from my bag and sharpen one of the pencils I always carry with me. I kneel on the floor, lay the open book on the bed, and begin to write:

24th December 1992

Dear Calippa
The only thing that makes you and me different from the people around us is that we've both been forced to acknowledge the truth. We both know that we're lost. You're lost forever in a crowded store on Christmas Eve 1976 – abandoned by parents too absorbed in what they're doing to even notice that you're missing and surrounded by people too intent on distracting themselves from the truth by spending money they don't have and buying things they don't need to give to other people they probably don't even like.
And I'm lost on Christmas Eve sixteen years later in a place where the beauty of the natural world fools people into believing that there might be some meaning in things, that there might be a divine being who actually cares about them, that their lives might actually

matter. They don't seem to realise that behind the façade of beauty and the impression of ordered design there's absolutely nothing. Or maybe something worse than nothing. Something malignant and destructive. Right now, I'm not sure whether their deluded state of mind makes me want to laugh or cry.

In fact, I'm no longer sure about anything. I'm not even sure at this moment if I want to go on living. But if I do manage to hang on to life, I think it will only be by accepting that there is nothing on which I can rely and no one in whom I can trust. Like you, I'm on my own and I'll just have to make the best of it. When I was younger, I thought my father was the person I could count on. He turned out to be a cheat and a liar. Nothing like the person I thought he was. My mother is weak and unreliable and her sister, my Auntie Cheryl, is not much better. Reuben's parents are well meaning and decent but understand almost nothing. Uncle Rob is as decent a human being as I have met, but right now I'm too afraid to trust even him. To have my hopes dashed again would be too much to bear.

And then there is – there was! – Reuben. I thought that he'd changed everything, that all my fears were groundless, that we really had found each other, that if we were lost we'd at least be lost together, that we'd be able to cling to each other for support – which I guess is what love is. But I should have known better. People like Reuben are an aberration. They appear out of nowhere and they disappear just as quickly. Lost without trace. They don't really fit into this world.

And one way or another, sooner or later, the world will find a way to be rid of them.

I don't know if these rambling thoughts mean anything at all. But then, I don't know if anything means anything at all. Tomorrow will be Christmas Day. I remember when I was a child and I was too excited about what the morning would bring to be able to sleep on this night. But tonight I'm dreading the thought of what tomorrow will be like. I don't care if I never see the morning. I'm just dead tired and I want to go to sleep and not wake up again.

Lori

I close the exercise book, drop it on the floor and turn off the light. The darkness floods the room and I fall into bed. Sleep comes fitfully and in my dreams I'm a child again, standing by the side of a lake and holding hands with another child. A little girl with blonde, curly hair. We're watching in horror as a succession of people run into the lake and then disappear from sight beneath its slate-grey water.

6
Christmas Eve 1996
Miss Bloom, do you believe that...

I'm carrying a heavy shopping bag in each hand and struggling to cross the busy Holloway Road in Islington before the traffic lights change again, when I hear a familiar voice calling my name and the sound of footsteps hurrying behind me.

'I wasn't sure if it was you, Miss. First time I've ever seen you out of school. Let me carry one of your bags for you.'

The speaker is a little out of breath, but one glimpse of his face is enough to tell me that his rapid breathing is due at least as much to his sheer excitement at our chance meeting as to his exertions in catching up with me. Goodness knows how far away he was when he first caught sight of me and how long he's been running after me. And by the time I reach the other side of the road, a delighted Leroy Williams, still unable to believe his good fortune in spotting his teacher in the street at three o'clock on Christmas Eve, has fallen into step alongside me. He stops for a moment to get his breath back and to take one of my shopping bags from me. This is an opportunity he's not about to miss.

'I'm really glad I've seen you, Miss Bloom. Got something to *axe* you…'

Leroy's an unusually interesting and clever thirteen-year-old with the ability of a born actor to switch his Caribbean accent on and off at will, depending on his audience and the impression he wants to make. But he always uses the distinctive pronunciation *axe* rather than the more usual *ask*. When I tried to suggest to him one day in class that he should correct this, he shook his head sagely and informed me with an authority beyond his years that his grandfather, who'd always spent the afternoon in the library on his day off from driving a London bus, had checked it out and that *axe* had been in common usage in that sense for centuries. In fact, he told me confidently, it was to be found in the very first English translation of the Bible.

He was so sure about his answer that I decided not to argue just in case he was right. I keep meaning to check if he was telling the truth or just getting one over on me. I wouldn't be the first of his teachers he's caught out in that way.

His grandfather, now in his late nineties, arrived in this country from Jamaica back in 1948, one of those original 492 passengers who disembarked at Tilbury from the HMT *Empire Windrush*. And his father, Joseph, is a Pentecostal pastor who leads a flock made up mainly of people who share his Caribbean heritage. They meet in a Gothic Revival-style building just off the Holloway Road. Its solemn and dreary-looking exterior stands in stark contrast to the uninhibited and spontaneous style of worship of the congregation inside. It was once an Anglican church with a typical London working-class congregation before the influx of immigrants and the subsequent flight of the indigenous white residents to the more affluent suburbs changed the make-up of the neighbourhood.

The kids at school, whatever their ethnic origins or religious background, are always pleased when Leroy's dad turns up to lead a morning assembly. Few of them come from families with any formal involvement in church. But they know that 'boring' is not a word you can legitimately use to describe Pastor Joseph's kind of Christianity.

And Leroy, the third-generation first-born male in this family is, as I say, an interesting character. I've got to know him since I became his English teacher back in September. He's the brightest kid in the class, though I have to be careful that I don't allow him to take over the entire lesson with his questions and opinions. He's inherited his grandfather's thirst for knowledge and his father's ability to hold the attention of an audience.

Unlike them, however, Leroy's goal is not merely to learn. Nor is it just to persuade or convert you. With Leroy, despite his youthfulness and apparent innocence, you always have to be alert. He has a knack for asking questions that catch you off guard and probe deeper than you first realise. A way of uncovering who you really are and exposing what you're really thinking. We were talking about it in the staffroom just before the end of term and agreeing that it's an unnerving talent in someone of his age. An ability all the trickier to deal with given that he's a thoroughly likeable boy without a hint of malice in his constant questioning. All the same, there isn't one of his teachers who isn't at least a little nervous of his interrogation.

We haven't walked more than a hundred yards before he launches into his question.

'You know that song we were all singing on the last morning before we broke up? What d'you think of it?' He slows his step and turns his head towards me. And I'm telling myself that it's ridiculous for me to be nervous in the presence of one of my pupils. He seems to sense that he's got the upper hand. 'Miss Bloom, do you believe that stuff? I tried to axe you in class. But you didn't really tell us what you thought.'

There had been something of a party atmosphere on the last day of term and the kids had been singing a variety of songs from the charts before we went into the school hall for the final assembly. I can't immediately think what song he's referring to.

'You know,' he says impatiently when he sees the puzzled expression on my face. 'The Dunblane song – "Knockin' on Heaven's Door".'

Then I realise what he's talking about. It's the version of Bob Dylan's song that's become an unlikely chart-topper throughout December. The Scottish singer, Ted Christopher, has added a new verse in memory of the five-and six-year-olds and their teacher who were shot and killed in Dunblane back in March when a gunman walked into their school and fired indiscriminately. A choir of some of the children who survived the attack provides the backing, and it's struck a chord around the country and raised significant funds for a number of charities. To the surprise of those of us on the teaching staff, it became something of an anthem at Holloway Road Secondary during the last couple of weeks of the term. But it was strange to hear groups of pupils singing about a town that would never be the same again after such a terrible loss. And it was certainly a change from the kinds of songs that normally grab their attention and get them singing at this time of year.

Now I'm struggling to know how to reply. And I'm annoyed with myself for being flummoxed by the question of a thirteen-year-old pupil who's spotted me by chance on my way home to get ready for my friends who'll be arriving for drinks and dinner at six o'clock. I want to tell him it's none of his business what I think. Or that I've never listened properly to the song. Or that walking down the Holloway Road on Christmas Eve really is neither the place nor the time for answering such a question. But I don't say any of those things. I just try to evade the question.

'Well, I'm not really sure what you mean by "that stuff". It's not really my kind of song, Leroy. But it's a very nice way to remember the children who were killed. And it's helped raise money for some good causes. So that's got to be good. And you all seem to like it.'

He gives me a half-smile. I can see from his expression that he knows I'm just being patronising. And he's not about to be put off so easily.

'Yeah, I agree, Miss. It is a nice song. But it's about God watching over those kids even when the man with the gun walked into the school. And about them being in heaven now. That's the stuff I mean. Do you believe that?'

We reach the corner where Fulton Road turns off the Holloway Road. Mercifully, I have the opportunity to escape before I have to answer the question.

'Well that *is* an interesting question,' I say with barely concealed relief. 'But it'll have to wait for another day I'm afraid, Leroy, since I'm nearly home. But it's been very nice to meet you. Thank you for carrying my bag for me. Please give my regards to your mum and dad. And I hope you'll have a lovely Christmas with your family.'

Leroy grins and concedes defeat. He knows he's been thwarted this time. But he has one last shot to fire before he hands my shopping bag back to me.

'And you too, Miss Bloom. And you should come to our New Year service at our church. You always say that you like my dad's assemblies at school. So I know you'll like this. It's even better. It lasts a bit longer than one of the assemblies and the music is really good.'

He digs in his jacket pocket and pulls out a slightly crumpled invitation to 'Begin a God-shaped New Year at the Fellowship of the Ransomed Church'. I thank him for it as I turn away and walk quickly to number 19 Fulton Road, annoyed that I can't get his questions out of my head.

The wrought-iron gate gives its familiar creaking sound as I push it open and step cautiously down the six uneven stone steps to the basement flat I've been renting for the past eighteen months. It's no mansion, and it definitely doesn't compare to the house I loved at 17 Morley Road in Bristol or to Cumberland Cottage with its view over Wythmere. But it's comfortable and clean and damp-free, and it's affordable on a teacher's salary. And the familiar tick of the old station waiting room clock hanging on the wall to my right just inside the door always makes me feel that, despite the time that's passed and what's been lost, this is my home.

I'm really fortunate in that Max Lawson who owns the property is a builder who runs his own small business, employing two or three tradesmen men doing extensions and renovations. So he's always quick to send someone round when there's a repair needing to be done. He even called round himself a week or two ago to install a new window that needed to be fitted quickly. I really liked him. He was telling me that his wife, whose mental health has been fragile for years, spends long periods in hospital. They don't have any children and I think his work has taken the place of family. I'm guessing that he must be in his late forties or early fifties, but he's a very attractive man for his age. In a fatherly sort of way, I mean.

I've been living here since I got the job at Holloway Road Secondary after completing my degree and my year of teacher training. Originally I had hoped to stay on at St Andrews and do postgraduate studies in English literature. But it took me a long time to get over Reuben's death and I found it hard to settle back into academic life and apply myself to study. Inevitably, my results weren't nearly good enough for me to be accepted for a doctoral research degree. Teaching in an inner-city London school was the last thing I'd ever imagined myself doing, but it's turned out to be the best thing I could have done. And, to my surprise, I actually enjoy teaching. A lot of the kids in my English classes are from deprived backgrounds and some of them have issues that show up in real behavioural problems. So the job can be demanding and even exhausting at times. But I feel like I'm doing something worthwhile, something that is making a difference to their lives.

Just as important, it doesn't leave me any time to brood over the past. The sleepless nights I had for the first eighteen months after Reuben's death and that left me constantly exhausted emotionally and physically are just a memory. My life has a settled routine these days. By the time I get home in an evening, make myself something to eat and finish whatever marking or preparation needs to be done for the next day, I'm usually ready to fall into bed by ten o'clock. I'm asleep as soon as my head hits the pillow, and even the constant rumble of the traffic going up and down the Holloway Road doesn't wake me. But the holidays provide a welcome break from the normal routine. This morning I took advantage of the opportunity to turn off the alarm and go back to sleep for another couple of hours. A blissful state for any hard-working schoolteacher.

Now I'm about to cook dinner for my three closest friends from school who'll be arriving at six o'clock. Devon and Chantelle are very much an item, but they've gone out of their way to befriend me, even spending two days of their precious half-term break helping me to decorate my flat. He teaches geography and she's one half of the school's music department. They met when they joined the staff at Holloway Road Secondary in August 1994, fell madly in love after trying to ignore each other for almost a year, and moved in together at the start of the autumn term. They're talking about getting married and starting a family when they can get enough money together to put down a deposit on a house.

Juliette's single and from Paris. She graduated from the Sorbonne with an outstanding degree and could be doing something that would earn her a lot more money than she's earning now. But she says that teaching French to inner-city London kids is an experience she wouldn't have missed for the world. She's not only highly intelligent, she's also one of the most beautiful women I've ever seen. To watch her in front of a class of normally rowdy sixteen-year-old boys is a sight to behold. They sit spellbound and open-mouthed, transfixed by her every word and following her every movement. We sometimes tease her by suggesting that while she maintains discipline better than anyone else on the staff, we doubt whether any of those boys is actually able to learn anything in such a state of near-hypnosis.

To say that Juliette and I have struck up a close friendship doesn't really do justice to the bond between us. She's become the sister I never had. A genuine *confidante*, the first person I've been able to trust and confide in since I lost Reuben. My mother and Uncle Rob still keep in close contact with me, of course. And even Auntie Cheryl and the Hodgsons call me from time to time and want to be helpful. But they're all part of a past that is still too raw for me to return to. Each year they plead with me to spend Christmas with them at Cumberland Cottage. And each year, despite my reluctance to inflict yet more hurt on them, I politely but steadfastly decline. I make sure that I take a trip north and spend a week or so travelling somewhere in the UK with them every summer, but I'm always glad to get back to the hustle and bustle of life in London. I'm never quite sure whether I'm trying to carve out a new identity or simply seeking to lose myself in the anonymity of the sprawling metropolis.

Juliette came to London after the break-up of a long-term relationship, determined to be an independent single woman in a new country for the foreseeable future. There have been more than a few eligible young men who've been captivated by her striking appearance and who've vied with each other for her affections. But whenever things show signs of getting serious, she quickly extricates herself from any further involvement. And when I ask her what's gone wrong this time, she'll always give me a swift analysis of the strengths and weaknesses of the latest rejected suitor before concluding with a Gallic shrug, '*J'ai endurci mon coeur.*' And that ability to put emotions on one side and look dispassionately at the situation is part of what's made her such an invaluable companion. As we've got to know each other better, I've even been able to open up to her about the loss of Reuben and the gaping hole that it's left in my life. She just listens quietly, pours us both a glass of wine and resists any temptation to offer the usual platitudes.

She's also been a great practical support. The excruciating period pains that are the bane of my life continue with that same relentless monthly rhythm that has plagued me since my teenage years. If anything, the discomfort is worse than ever. Several visits to my GP have been of little help, and I leave each time with the impression that he thinks I'm just a rather weak female making a fuss about some mild irritation that's just part and parcel of life for every other woman. There have been one or two days when the pain has been so bad that I've had to walk out of the class I've been teaching and lie down in the staffroom. And each time Juliette's had a free period – no pun intended – and has gone straight in to cover for me. She's also been trying to persuade me to put some pressure on my doctor to arrange an appointment with a gynaecological specialist.

'The problem with you English women,' she says, 'is that you're too nice and too willing to put up with things. Let me come with you next time you go. We'll make that man sit up and take notice…'

If things don't improve, I may just take her up on that offer. But for now, although I haven't inherited my mother's ability as a cook and my culinary skills are strictly limited, I'm glad to be entertaining such good friends. I've no doubt that the dessert Devon and Chantelle have made and the wine Juliette will bring will more than make up for my very ordinary offering. I'm doing a butternut squash soup with bacon for starters, which should at least warm everyone up. And my lemon basil shrimp risotto usually turns out alright, and sometimes even makes guests think I'm more competent in the kitchen than I really am.

Right on six o'clock, the doorbell rings and the three of them arrive together. We're all too hungry to waste time on small talk before we sit down to eat and the meal goes better than I could have hoped. There are even some compliments on my cooking which, since we're only on the first glass of wine, actually seem to me to be genuine. Devon apologises for the fact that his attempt at making a Caribbean rum cake ended in disaster while Chantelle just shakes her head and says she tried to tell him he was doing it all wrong but, typical man that he is, he just wouldn't listen. However, a little thing like that isn't going to spoil our evening and we all agree that the chocolate mousse they've picked up at the supermarket on the way is a very acceptable dessert. And after several glasses of the excellent wine that Juliette has brought, we begin to relax into the evening as the warm glow of friendship fills the room and the conversation flows smoothly. That's when I tell them about meeting Leroy Williams on the way home that afternoon.

'He's a funny kid,' Chantelle says when I've finished the story of my unexpected encounter. 'Devon's folks go to the Fellowship of the Ransomed Church. And they've told us that everyone thinks his dad's already grooming him to take over the leadership of the church in the future. Sees him as a budding evangelist. So he'll be glad to know that his son's been asking you such leading questions and inviting you to the church.'

Devon shakes his head before pouring himself another glass of wine. He's clearly not convinced that this succession plan is likely to meet with success.

'Hmm... Somehow, I don't see Leroy being the next in line in the Williams family Pentecostal dynasty. He's too much of a free spirit. One of the other kids who goes to FORC says that Williams junior was asked to step out of a youth Bible study just the other week for daring to disagree with his dad over some point of doctrine. He's much more interested in provoking a reaction in people than pastoring a flock. He'd have the congregation in a state of high anxiety before the end of his first year in the pulpit.'

There's general agreement with Devon's observation, and that seems to draw a line under the topic of Leroy and his probing questions. I'm already starting to look through my CD collection, thinking that a little mellow background music and a few more glasses of red wine will help create the perfect ambience for a long, lazy evening of easy and undemanding conversation.

Juliette, however, has other ideas.

'You know what – why don't we talk about Leroy's question? I know there's only four of us here, but we're an interesting group, if you think about it. I mean, I'm French, nominally Catholic, I suppose. But really I've got a completely secular mindset. Devon and Chantelle, you've drifted away from the very vibrant kind of faith of your parents. But that's where your roots are and it must still impact you in some ways. And, Lori, you're like a lot of English people. If you had to declare some kind of religious faith on an official document, you'd probably write down "Anglican". But I know from what you've told me about yourself that for you it's more a part of the cultural backdrop to your life rather than anything that's significant.'

The room goes quiet. I put down the CDs that I'm holding and look at the others, half-expecting someone to pooh-pooh the suggestion and object that it's far too serious a topic of conversation for Christmas Eve. But

Chantelle, who's normally the quietest and most reticent of the four of us, breaks the silence.

'Funny you should say that, Juliette.' She gives Devon a knowing glance that he returns with a slightly embarrassed smile. 'And we might as well tell you the truth. The reason the cake went all wrong is that we were having a bit of an argument this afternoon and forgot all about it until we smelt the burning. For a while now I've been saying that when we start a family we need to go back to church again, because I think kids should have a grounding in faith until they're old enough to choose for themselves. But Devon's folks were very strict with him. Probably a bit too strict. He found church a bit of a suffocating place to be. Says he'd be a hypocrite if he went back and that he thinks there are other ways to teach a child about faith and spirituality. It's become a real bone of contention between us. So maybe you two single women can help us with a more objective view of things.'

Even Juliette is surprised that her suggestion has been taken up so readily and that we're already right in the middle of a serious discussion. For the next twenty minutes we discuss Devon and Chantelle's dilemma, recognising both sides of the argument without arriving at any definite conclusion. But despite our failure to resolve the issue, they obviously feel better for having aired the problem. It seems like the right time to get up and make coffee.

I fill everyone's cup and assume that the combination of caffeine and alcohol will relax us and ease us back into small talk. But Devon doesn't think it's fair that all of the attention has been on him and Chantelle and their as yet unborn offspring.

'Hang on,' he says after a sip of coffee. 'Very nice of you both to give us the benefit of your wisdom on how to bring up children we don't even have yet. But, Lori, we still don't know *your* answer to Leroy's question. *Do* you believe that stuff? *Do* you believe that God's watching over us? Even when things go wrong…'

'Well,' I respond after a moment's pause, 'I certainly know what it's like when that happens, when everything goes wrong…'

Juliette and I have had long conversations over the last year in which we've talked in detail about the painful times in my life. However, I've never shared these things with Devon and Chantelle. I sense that Juliette's watching me, concerned for me and ready to step in and steer the conversation in another direction if I show any signs of being uncomfortable. Looking back, I don't know whether it was the wine loosening my tongue and breaking down my customary inhibitions, or if it was just the right moment for me to be open and honest about my life, but almost before I realise what's happening, I find myself responding to Devon's observations by relating my experiences of 'when things go wrong' – discovering my father's deception, living through my parents' divorce after he went to prison, and, of course, having to come to terms with the death of Reuben. I leave nothing out. And when I reach the end of my tale, I'm ready to state my position.

'So, Devon, I'm something of an expert on the topic of everything going wrong. But the answer's no. I don't believe that stuff. There was nobody watching my dad or doing anything to stop him when he was living a double life, cheating on my mother and me and breaking the law of the land. And there was nobody watching over Reuben when he was gasping for breath and struggling for his life in Wythmere. I've got nothing against those who do believe in a God who's looking after them and in a heaven where those you've loved and lost go to when they die. If people find some kind of comfort in that, if it helps them carry on and get through life, I'm the last person to criticise or condemn them. I know how hard it is to keep going. I'm grateful for my family, for friends like you, for work that keeps me busy, for some light in the darkness that makes me want to keep on living and hoping. But I don't believe and I'm certainly not knocking on heaven's door.'

I stop, suddenly aware that the room is silent and that the others have been listening intently to everything I've been saying. The relaxed party atmosphere has completely dissipated. A wave of embarrassment sweeps over me and I remind myself that it's Christmas Eve and that I should be playing the role of the happy hostess. I try to lighten the mood with what I hope is a witty comment.

'Well, knowing my luck, I don't think there'd be anybody at home to answer it even if such a door existed.' And then, feeling my eyes stinging and the tears beginning to well up, I quickly add, 'You know what, I think I need some more coffee. I've obviously had way more wine than is good for me and it's making me maudlin and weepy.'

I stand up, take hold of the tray with the coffee pot and the cups, intending to busy myself in the kitchen until I get a hold on my emotions. But Devon takes the tray out of my hands.

'Sit down, Lori. You've done enough already making dinner. And that was incredibly brave of you to tell us all that. We'd no idea that you'd come through such tragedy. Let me see to the coffee. I'm sure you three ladies can manage without my manly wisdom while I prove to Chantelle that I can at least make a decent cup of coffee.' He pauses briefly and glances at me, as if he's uncertain about what he's about to add. 'But when I come back, I want to ask you another question, if you don't mind. We don't get enough chances for real conversation like this.'

He emerges from the kitchen ten minutes later looking rather pleased with himself and carrying the tray with the coffee pot and cups neatly set out beside a plate of biscuits and four serviettes neatly arranged. Chantelle jokingly chides him about the fact that he never demonstrates such attention to presentation at home, and that leads to some good-natured banter between them. I'm hoping he'll have forgotten about whatever the question was that he wanted to ask me. But as soon as he's poured the coffee and passed the cups around it's clear that it hasn't slipped from his mind.

'So, Lori,' he says setting his cup down and looking straight at me. 'Tell me to mind my own business if you want. But clearly you've come through some difficult times, to put it mildly. You're not religious, obviously, but you've managed to hold things together and move on with life. You must be finding some kind of comfort or strength somewhere. Some sort of purpose. Something that gives you a reason to live…'

He doesn't round off his question properly. Just lets his words hang in the air. And somehow the silence that follows makes it impossible for me to avoid giving him an answer, even though it suddenly occurs to me that this is a question I've never allowed myself to think about. Now I'm asking myself, 'What is it that keeps me going?'

When I do speak, I realise that I'm thinking aloud, searching in my mind for an answer rather than telling him something I already know. And what comes out of my mouth takes me by surprise.

'Well, I guess what keeps me sane and helps me keep going is my friend, Calippa Cumberland.' I stop and smile at their puzzled expressions and repeat the name. 'Yes, it's *Calippa Cumberland*. Funny name, I know. I think I probably misheard it. But that's who she'll always be in my mind. She's been a friend since childhood and I used to talk to her almost every night. Quite often during the day as well, now I come to think of it. These days we don't talk nearly so much, but I write to her regularly. And interestingly enough, it's twenty years ago to the day since I met her.'

And then, for the first time in those twenty years, I hear myself telling three other adults outside my immediate family about my encounter with the little lost girl with the blonde curls crying for her parents on Christmas Eve 1976. About my childish fears that she'd be wandering alone through Kendrew's Department Store in Bristol forever. About the long conversations I used to have with her walking to and fro along the garden wall in Morley Road. About the dozens of lined blue exercise books I keep locked safely away and which provide a commentary on both the trivial everyday happenings and the more significant events in my life, all written painstakingly in pencil on page after page.

'Now if you think I'm really weird and you want to leave now, I'd fully understand,' I say with a wry chuckle as I reach the end of my story. 'But even as I'm trying to explain it to you, I can see more clearly than ever just how important my imaginary friend has been to me. Still is, for that matter. It was my natural childish sympathy for her plight that started it all off. But it's obviously become something much deeper than that. I guess it'd be interesting to find out what a psychologist would make of it. On second thoughts, it's probably better not to know. They might want to lock me up for my own safety!'

The room has gone very quiet and I can sense that the others are weighing up how to respond to this unexpected revelation of my ongoing twenty-year relationship with an imaginary childhood friend. For a moment I wonder if I've made a mistake in sharing something so personal and admittedly unusual, and I can feel my face beginning to flush with embarrassment. I'm relieved when Devon comes to my rescue.

'Wow! I didn't expect that when I asked you my question. But this is a lot more interesting than just making small talk and whiling the evening away. I'm no psychologist, but it *is* very interesting – maybe significant's a better way to put it – that you've been confiding in someone who's been…' he struggles to find the right words, '… well, someone who's been permanently lost since childhood.'

'I know, I know,' I protest. 'I think you're being kind describing it as "interesting". It's positively weird. I've wondered about it myself. I keep thinking of a bit of Shakespeare. A line from *The Tempest* – "misery acquaints a man with strange bedfellows". I'm not miserable – at least, not all the time! And I think people who know me like you do see me as being fairly normal and reasonably happy. But I think I've always felt a little bit lost, never quite sure of my place in the world or what life is all about. And that became all the more acute after my parents' divorce and Reuben's death. Maybe that's why it's been helpful to share my feelings with someone else who knows what it's like to be lost. Even if that someone exists only in my imagination. I guess an imaginary friend from childhood is a strange bedfellow for somebody in their mid-twenties.'

'Well, I'm not sure that it is all *that* odd, if you really think about it.'

Juliette is looking at me with an expression on her face that's halfway between thoughtfulness and scepticism.

'I mean, is it all *that* different from what believers do when they pray? Aren't *they* talking to someone they can't see? And certainly within the Christian tradition, to a considerable degree, their urge to pray comes from a sense of their own lostness. And their faith that their prayers can help reflects their conviction that the person to whom they're speaking has experienced that same sense of lostness or something even worse. You know – Jesus on the cross asking God why he's forsaken him…' She shrugs and seems to run out of words. 'Oh well, at least all those religious instruction classes I sat through as a child weren't entirely wasted.'

We talk for another hour. It's the kind of conversation that we don't often have time or space for. The kind of conversation in which we share honestly and openly in the way you can only do with people you really trust. The kind of conversation that comes to a quiet end, not because you've exhausted the topic or found all the answers, but because you've said as much as you can say about it at this moment. The kind of conversation that ends in reflective silence as we sit around, comfortable in each other's company and grateful for each other's friendship. We sit for a full five minutes and none of us can quite think of what to do or say until Juliette suddenly stands up.

'Do you know what I think is *la chose la plus importante* about what Lori has told us?'

Juliette often throws in a little bit of French when she thinks she's saying something of particular significance. We laugh at her and tell her that it makes her sound like Inspector Poirot, which tends to annoy her as she insists that, since he is Belgian, his accent is subtly but distinctly different from hers. She also likes to answer her own questions. So we resist the temptation to laugh, and sit quietly waiting for what she's about to say.

'Well, I'll tell you. It's about how important the things are that happen to you when you're a child. I don't just mean things like learning to write or add up. I mean the things that touch something deep inside you. Lori, your imaginary childhood friend still has a place in your life because she helps you to deal with things that otherwise might be covered up and allowed to fester. And what you've just told us is stirring an old memory in me…'

She hesitates for a moment and I find myself both intrigued and slightly uncomfortable. Juliette has a habit of picking up something that's been said and taking the conversation in a completely unexpected direction.

'My family wasn't religious,' she continues. 'Not what you'd call practising Catholics. But when I was a child we used to go to church every year on Christmas Eve. I couldn't understand everything. In fact, not understanding everything was a big part of what made it so special. It was wonderful, mysterious – all the bells and smells and the choir singing and the liturgy in Latin that I couldn't understand – and it touched something deep inside me.'

'I know what you mean,' Chantelle interjected. 'Our church was very different from what yours would have been, Juliette. But I loved Christmas Eve. The thought of a baby being born in a stable always made me cry…'

'*Exactement*,' Juliette responds. She always reverts to her native tongue and uses that word when she thinks she's on the verge of clinching her argument. 'That's what I was about to say. I'm thinking that the baby in the crib at the front of the church had the same effect on me and on you, Chantelle, that the lost little girl in the department store had on Lori. I felt sorry for a family locked out of the inn and the newborn baby lying in a cattle trough.'

I'm not quite convinced by her reasoning, though Devon and Chantelle seem to be persuaded. It doesn't quite feel like an apt parallel to me. But we've had enough serious conversation for one evening, so I stifle my urge to disagree and decide to leave it there. Juliette, however, is not finished.

'So why don't we all put our coats on and head to a church where they're having a proper Christmas Eve service? You know, the kind where you get to sing carols by candlelight. Just for old time's sake. See if it still has the same effect on us…'

I protest that I don't do church. That the last time I attended a church service was Reuben's funeral and that was not an experience I want to remember, for all sorts of reasons. But my three friends think it'll be just the right way to round off what's been a perfect evening. I try suggesting that they should go without me and I'll stay at home, a proposal they reject out of hand. There's no way they'll leave me on my own, they counter. And, in the end, I reluctantly agree to go with them to the parish church at the far end of Fulton Road.

By the time we've reached a decision and got ourselves out of the house it's gone eleven o'clock and I'm hoping that the service will have started. Maybe it'll be the kind of church where they're strict about that kind of thing and they'll refuse to let us in.

We get to St Austen's at quarter past eleven and, as I'd been hoping, the service is indeed under way if the sound of singing is anything to go by. I've almost managed to persuade my companions that the priest might be about to pray and that it would be irreverent and disrespectful to walk in now, when an elderly lady standing in the porch spots us. I immediately take a liking to her, as she looks exactly as I would have loved my grandmothers to have looked had they not died before I was born. She's silver-haired and ruddy-cheeked with a smile that sends out a cheerful glow. And she's dressed in a serviceable tweed coat that was designed with warmth rather than style in mind, a woolly hat that reminds me of an old tea cosy we used to have when I was a child, and thick black stockings. Best of all, on her feet she's wearing what I can only describe as perfect 'grandma shoes' – stout, comfortable, highly polished, black lace-ups with a low block heel in a broad fitting, designed, no doubt, to accommodate the bunions that often come with much walking and the passing of many years.

It's immediately obvious that she's been assigned to look out for latecomers like us, and she welcomes us enthusiastically with a cheery greeting before thrusting into our hands an A4 sheet of paper with half a dozen carols printed on it and an unlit candle fitted into a little paper cup.

'I'm so sorry we're late,' I hear myself apologising. 'I hope we won't disturb anyone by going in now.'

'Oh, don't worry about that, my dear,' she replies, smiling at my embarrassment and patting the back of my hand. 'You're very welcome. We always get a few latecomers on Christmas Eve. People often get us confused with St Anthony's. Did you and your friends get lost on the way?'

Her question makes Juliette smile. She looks at me and winks, and then turns back to the elderly white-haired lady and says, 'Yes, I guess you could say that. One of her friends got lost…'

7
Christmas Eve 2000
Just be careful, Lori, my dear…

This will be the first Christmas Eve since 1996 that I haven't had Juliette and the Campbells here for dinner. Juliette is in France for her sister's wedding. And now that their little boy, Daniel, is almost two years old, Devon and Chantelle have reached that stage where they're having to allocate their time evenly between both sets of doting grandparents over the festive season.

It will feel odd not having them here and not heading off to the carol service at St Austen's just before eleven o'clock. To my surprise, it's become something of a Christmas Eve ritual that I actually look forward to and enjoy. The same silver-haired elderly lady hands us a carol sheet as we enter and always greets us with the same words: 'Welcome to St Austen's. I'm Margherita Timmins, but everyone calls me Madge. Please feel at home.' I'm sure she must be in her mid to late seventies, but she's one of those elderly people who appear to be full of energy and who give the impression of being indestructible. She always recognises us – even remembering our names from one year to the next – and always seems genuinely pleased to welcome us. I'll miss seeing her tonight. For Juliette and me, it's still our one annual visit to church, though Devon and Chantelle have become regulars at the Fellowship of the Ransomed Church each Sunday and valued members of Pastor Joseph Williams' congregation.

But I won't be home alone this evening. Max Lawson is coming round for dinner. To be honest, he spends as much time here as he does at his own place these days. In the spring of last year, he decided that although I was happy enough with things as they were, he wanted to upgrade the apartment. He said I was such a good tenant that he wanted to make sure I didn't go anywhere else. And he really went to town on the job – rebuilding the steps down to the front door, rewiring throughout, fitting a new central heating system, knocking down an interior wall, replacing a window, plastering and painting – far beyond anything I'd expected. The work took almost three months, and he did most of it himself. The five men he employs were too busy with other stuff, he explained. And anyhow, as he often reminded me, he spent too many hours of his life doing business admin and filling in tax returns. So this was 'a labour of love' and it would help him keep his hand in.

I guess that's when our friendship began to develop. As the evenings lengthened, he'd work on a little later each week, I'd make dinner for him and we'd sit chatting until it was dark outside. Since the first day I met him, I've found him attractive. But the age difference between us – more than twenty-five years – made me feel safe. I'd told myself that it would be a long time, if ever, before I could even think about a relationship with a man that went beyond friendship. And Max, after all, was old enough to be my father. In fact, in those long conversations we had, he became in a way the father I never had. He listened when I needed to talk, he put an arm around me when I was tired or despondent, and he encouraged me to keep up my links with my mother and Uncle Rob when I might simply have lost contact with them.

But I know when it all changed, when it became something more than friendship, more than a father–daughter relationship. The summer term at school had ended, Max had put the final touches to the work he'd done on the apartment, and we decided that we should mark its completion with a celebration. He wanted to take me out to a nice restaurant for a fancy dinner. But I protested that since he'd done so much for me, I'd like to make a special meal for him.

I consulted with Juliette, who's a much better cook than I am, about what I could make that would be worthy of such a special occasion but within the range of my limited abilities. She seemed unusually reluctant to help me and I could tell there was something troubling her. In the end, I asked her straight out what was in her mind that she wasn't putting into words. As soon as she started speaking I wished I hadn't been so keen to find out.

'Lori, are you sure you know what you're getting yourself into here? You're spending a lot of time with a man who's so much older than you are. And what's more important, he's a man with a wife, a wife who spends long periods at a time in mental institutions. I think there's more in this relationship than you're admitting to yourself. I'm worried that you could be getting yourself into something that could turn out to be complicated and messy. I'm worrying that you're going to get hurt.'

I protested angrily that her suggestion was utterly ridiculous. The conversation became heated and ended abruptly. For a time we avoided each other. And for the next week I tried to tell myself that her fears were unfounded. But the more I did so, the more I began to realise just how strong my feelings for Max had become. If Juliette's words had been meant to warn me off, they actually had the opposite effect of bringing my true feelings to the surface. And the more I faced the truth, the more determined I became to allow my emotions to lead me wherever they would.

Fate had robbed me of Reuben Hodgson. There would never be anyone who could take his place. But maybe I could love and be loved again. Of course, I couldn't be absolutely sure that Max felt the same way about me. But if he did, I wasn't going to allow myself to be robbed of this opportunity to grab some happiness and find love for the second time in my life. In the previous few years I'd had several brief relationships. What my mother would have a called a 'fling'. But they had been nothing more than sexual encounters, answering a physical need I couldn't ignore but bereft of any real emotional connection. This was different.

I think we both knew when we sat down to our romantic candle-lit dinner in my newly refurbished kitchen-diner that summer evening in 1999 how the night was going to end. The meal turned out better than I had dared to hope and the sound of Max's favourite singer, Frank Sinatra, crooning in the background helped to create the perfect ambience. We talked less than we normally did when we were together but we both knew what was in each other's thoughts.

There was a brief moment when I hesitated about the direction in which we were heading. Wondered if I might regret it and whether I ought to make some excuse and bring the evening to an end. But it passed quickly. And I knew that there was one thing I didn't have to worry about. I'd recently registered with a new GP practice where a very helpful young woman doctor had listened to me properly for the first time in my life. She put me on the pill to alleviate the unpleasantly heavy and painful periods I'd suffered since I was a teenager and which she diagnosed as being symptoms of endometriosis, a word I only vaguely recognised. It was a relief to have a possible diagnosis and some practical help after having been told for so long that I just needed to make less fuss and get on with things like other women did.

And as I sat looking at Max and thinking about what might be about to happen, I was glad that there was no fear of me getting pregnant and having my teaching career interrupted.

When the meal was over and we were sharing a third glass of wine, I made one last effort to appease my conscience by asking Max about his marriage.

'I don't want to be the kind of person who comes between a husband and wife,' I concluded. 'I'll understand if you want to leave now.'

He took hold of my hand and smiled at me. His marriage, he said, had been the greatest mistake of his life, that they hadn't shared a physical relationship for years, that he stayed with his wife only out of a sense of duty, fearing for what she might do to herself if he left her on her own.

'I made a promise that I'd make sure she'd always be looked after. And I'll never go back on that. But it's been a marriage in name only. I've thrown myself into the business just to keep myself busy and my mind occupied. And I really have tried to be faithful to her despite everything. In nearly thirty years I can honestly say that there have only been a couple of times when I've found some comfort with another woman. But what I've discovered since I met you… well, that's something different. I haven't felt alive like this since I was in my twenties.'

And that was it. The time for talking was over. We spent the night together as a couple. Just as we've done on so many nights since then. Our relationship isn't formalised in any way. And I don't think that it's common knowledge, though I'm sure my neighbours must draw their own conclusions when they see him arriving in the evening and leaving in the morning with me as I head to school. I've patched up my friendship with Juliette despite the fact that I know she's still unhappy about my friendship with Max and concerned about what the outcome might be. I haven't yet said anything to my mother. But I will tell her and Uncle Rob and Auntie Cheryl when I see them in a week's time, though I'll limit my information to saying only that I've got 'a partner who's very nice'. That's the kind of phrase they'll accept without asking too many questions.

They still invite me to spend Christmas with them at Cumberland Cottage every year. And every year I have to tell them that the memories remain too painful for me to do that. But we've reached a compromise by getting together every New Year's Eve. We meet up in a hotel just off the motorway this side of Birmingham, a venue we've chosen simply because it's a convenient halfway point for them and for me.

But tonight, on this cold and wintry Christmas Eve, I don't have to go anywhere beyond the front door of my apartment and I don't have to deal with any troublesome thoughts about how I'm going to explain my actions to anyone who might disapprove. It'll be just Max and me eating dinner together, then relaxing with a glass or two of wine and some suitable seasonal music before we head to bed.

He's coming straight from the hospital where he's been visiting his wife. Her mental health is such that there's little prospect of her leaving hospital any time soon, and he visits her faithfully two or three times every week.

Early in the relationship we talked about the possibility of him getting a divorce so that we could marry. But his Catholic upbringing and his sense that the emotional stress this would cause would be too much for her make this idea a non-starter. I fully understand that and I'm just grateful that he's part of my life. And, if I've learned anything in my almost twenty-eight years, it's that when the perfect is out of reach you don't turn down the chance of the next best thing.

The evening goes exactly as planned, and once we've settled together on the settee with just the lights from the

Christmas tree and the glow of the surprisingly convincing 'flames' coming from the rather expensive electric fire that Max insisted on installing when he did the renovations, I decide it's time to have a bit of fun. I eject the CD of seasonal songs we've been listening to and put on this year's Christmas number one, a song that's come out of left field and knocked even the boy band Westlife off the top of the charts. It's the theme music from an animated children's television series in which the favourite character, Bob, is a builder – just like Max. And anybody who's in the building trade is being driven crazy by having people chant the recurring refrain at them, asking if they think they can build it and responding with a loud response in the affirmative. Max groans as soon as he hears the music and tells me that he'll walk out on me immediately if it doesn't stop. And before I can turn it off, he adds with his hands clasped and an expression of mock piety on his face, 'And God, if You can hear me, please do something to rescue me from this terrible song.'

What happens next makes us both stop in our tracks. We look at each other in amazement before bursting into laughter. For no sooner are the words out of his mouth than we hear contrasting strains to those that are threatening to drive Max to distraction. It's the sound of carol singing coming from the street. We step outside and listen for a few minutes, appreciating the unanticipated blessing of music more appropriate for Christmas Eve.

Because we're standing in the doorway of a basement apartment and the pavement is just about at eye level, the first thing I notice is the singers' feet. And there's something familiar about the feet and ankles closest to me

– those thick black stockings and that stout black pair of highly polished leather lace-up shoes with their low block heel. It can only be one person, the person I thought I wouldn't see tonight.

I wait until the impromptu choir of just six or seven voices has finished its rendition of 'In the Bleak Midwinter' before I hurry up the steps to greet the wearer of this sturdy footwear.

'Madge Timmins, it's you! So good to see you. We're not able to be at the service tonight. And I was quite disappointed that I wouldn't get to wish you a Merry Christmas this year.'

I'm suddenly taken aback by the spontaneity and sincerity of my own words. I really do mean what I've just said, even though I hardly know this woman to whom I've spoken only briefly four times previously in the draughty porch of a church on the way in to a carol service. And then I get embarrassed about my eagerness to speak to her. It's night-time and she wouldn't have been expecting to see me. She probably won't even recognise me in the dark. Maybe she'll have forgotten me since last year.

'Lori, how lovely to see you. I'd no idea you lived here.' She certainly hasn't forgotten me and she throws her arms around me and gives me a hug. She seems as pleased to see me as I am to see her. 'And how odd we should stop right outside your house. We do our carol singing in a different street in the neighbourhood every Christmas Eve. I keep thinking I should really retire from the choir. But they keep persuading me to stay, and I enjoy it so much. And not everybody will be able or want to come to the Christmas Eve service. So it's nice to take a little bit of Christmas to them.'

By this time Max has come up the steps and is standing next to me. He nods at Madge Timmins, who returns his unspoken greeting with a smile of recognition.

'It's Mr Lawson, isn't it? You did the work on converting the old vicarage to a community centre at St Austen's two or three years ago. You did a good job for us. I remember you were very busy at that time and you were having to leave work to visit your wife in hospital most days. How is she doing? I hope she's much improved.'

Max nods again to confirm that he is who she thinks he is, tells her he's glad the congregation at St Austen's is pleased with work he did, and explains that the nature of his wife's illness means that she's unlikely ever to return home.

Madge listens sympathetically and tries to steer the conversation on to a happier topic. She's spotted that Max and I are not only standing together but that we've emerged from the same door and come up the same steps. And she's trying to figure out our relationship.

'So you two know each other, obviously,' she says innocently. Then an expression you might expect to see from someone who's just solved a tricky puzzle crosses her face. 'Of course, you're father and daughter, aren't you?'

I feel myself getting embarrassed and I'm unsure how to reply. But Max takes the question in his stride and responds with an easy laugh.

'No, no, we're not related. I'm afraid we were never blessed with children. And anyhow, Lori's way too good-looking to be my daughter. No, we're just very good friends. Despite the age difference.'

Madge Timmins may be long past the first flush of youth or even the years of middle age, but her mind is as sharp as ever. I can see from her reaction that she's grasped the situation and that she senses this is a line of enquiry it would be insensitive to pursue any further. She quickly changes the direction of the conversation without missing a step.

'Well, there's nothing like friendships with younger people to keep you youthful, I always say. And I know from how you always greet me, Lori, that you're comfortable talking with people a lot older than Mr Lawson.'

She smiles knowingly at me and I return her smile with a nod that I hope shows how grateful I am for her sensitivity.

'But my friends are halfway up the street, and I'd better get a move on or I'll be left behind,' she adds, before giving me another hug, pulling me close to her and whispering in my ear, 'Just be careful, Lori, my dear. Just be careful. And you know where you can find me if you ever want somebody who'll listen without bombarding you with advice. It's a long time ago, but I was your age once.'

She releases her hold on me, loudly wishes us a Merry Christmas and hurries off in pursuit of her fellow carollers, leaving me a little uncertain as to what to make of the brief exchange between us. Max and I make our way back indoors and try to pick up from where we'd left off. I put on a compilation CD of some of his favourite singers, snuggle up beside him on the couch and try to relax. But without really thinking about what I'm saying, I hear myself suggesting that we should go to the carol service at St Austen's. Max responds to my proposal with a look of incredulity.

'Are you serious? I'm just getting warm again after standing outside in the cold. And I've been looking forward to a relaxing evening.' His expression changes and he lowers his voice and pulls me closer. 'Well, maybe a *romantic* evening would be more truthful. And now you want us to get wrapped up and sit in a draughty church. Come on, Lori, be fair on a man…'

He knows how to put on that pleading voice that men resort to when their plans seem about to be thwarted. But I know that the way I'm feeling at the moment, I'm definitely not in the right frame of mind for his amorous advances. My feminine charms win out over his masculine stubbornness, and half an hour later we arrive at St Austen's to be greeted at the door by a delighted Madge Timmins. Unseen by Max, as she hands me the regulation carol sheet and the customary unlit candle fitted into a little paper cup, I slip a hastily handwritten note into her hand.

The church is full. Looking around, I guess that probably half the congregation, just like Max and me, are not regular attenders but have been brought here on this evening by a longing that is deeper than mere nostalgia for the wonder of Christmas Eves gone by. A persistent longing that they can neither fully understand nor clearly articulate for something that will slake an ever-present thirst that somehow becomes more acute at times like this. Like me, their head tells them that the trappings of religion belong to the past, a past to which they have no desire to return. But, for all that, their heart insists that without something more than the routine of life and the prospect of the years passing ever more quickly, the future is a place in which there is little hope of finding satisfaction.

I push those thoughts to the back of my mind and just lose myself in the carols I vaguely remember from childhood and in the company of people with whom I would otherwise have little in common. By the time we reach the point in the service where the church is plunged into darkness and we light our candles, I can see that even Max is beginning to thaw out emotionally, even if the heating system is proving to be less than adequate to properly warm the building.

We drop our extinguished candles with their little paper cups into a cardboard box as we file out of the church at the end of the service. And the vicar, no doubt heartened at such a full house, is glowing with *bonhomie* as he shakes us by the hand and wishes us 'a happy and blessed Christmas'. I wonder what the difference might be between those two adjectives but content myself with responding, 'You too, vicar.' He recognises Max from his time working on the church extension and greets him warmly. To my relief, he doesn't realise that we've come together. The prospect of explaining to a vicar that I'm not Max's daughter while standing in a line of people impatiently waiting to leave and go home just after midnight is not one that I would have relished.

Just as we step out of the church into the cold night air, Madge Timmins emerges from the shadows. She tries to pretend that it's a chance encounter, but I'm sure that she's been waiting for us quite intentionally.

'Glad I've bumped into you,' she says to Max, not entirely convincingly. 'I hope you've enjoyed the service. Lori and I only get to meet up once a year on Christmas Eve, but I always look forward to it.' As she says my name, she reaches out and squeezes my hand affectionately. 'So meeting you both twice this evening has been a bit of a treat for an old lady. Have a wonderful Christmas.'

And with that, she turns around and hurries off, leaving Max with a smile on his face and me with the note she's just slipped into my hand. I was right about her deliberately waiting for us. I drop the note into my coat pocket without mentioning it to Max.

'What a charming old lady,' he says as we begin to walk home hand in hand. 'I remember her being just the same when we were working at the church. Always around the place, busying herself with something, and always had the kettle on ready to make us a cup of tea. She's certainly taken a shine to you, especially considering that you only go to her church once a year on Christmas Eve.'

I have a momentary urge to tell him about what has passed between Madge Timmins and me that evening – our whispered conversation outside the house and the message I passed to her as we entered the church. I want to stop under the light of a street lamp and open her reply to me and read it aloud there and then. But I'm nervous of what it might say and of what the consequences of reading it to Max might be. So I resist that urge and decide that before I say anything to him, I'll share it with an old friend and see how I feel about it after that.

That's why, an hour after we've got home and gone to bed, I get up just after half past one, leaving Max fast asleep, put on my dressing gown, tiptoe into the front room and fumble in the pocket of my coat, which I deliberately left lying on the back of a chair. I take out the note that Madge Timmins pushed into my hand as we were leaving the church, unfold it carefully on the table in front of me and read what she's written.

Dear Lori

Thanks for your note. I slipped out of the church and into the vestry during the last carol to write this so that I could give it to you at the end of the service.

I don't know Max Lawson well, but my sense is that you're right about him. He is a decent man and life hasn't been easy for him with his wife's long illness. I know what you mean when you say that you're both people who've been robbed of the life and the love you'd expected would be yours. And I do understand how you feel – maybe more than you realise.

But it's clear from what you've told me that you're troubled about your relationship with Max for more than one reason. And, yes, I'd be happy to meet up with you. Just give me a call and we'll make a time to have a chat.

And by the way, I don't know if you believe in prayer. But I'll be praying for you anyway. As I often tell people, that certainly won't do any harm and it might just help.

Meanwhile I hope you have a peaceful Christmas.

Love

Madge

She's put her phone number in large letters at the bottom of the page and underscored it twice, as if she wants to make sure I don't miss it. I'll call her in a couple of days. But for now, I say the number over quietly to myself several times and try to commit it to memory. Then, still trying not to make a sound, I go over to the old sideboard I bought in a charity shop just after I moved in, open the bottom drawer where I keep the pile of blue-covered exercise books, and pick out the one lying on the top. As I set it down on the table and open it to a blank page, I can hear the ticking of the old station waiting room clock hanging by the door. It seems to be unusually loud and I have a sudden fear that Max will wake up and wonder why I'm out of bed. I hold my breath and sit absolutely still, but there's no sound of any movement from the bedroom. So I take one of the pencils I always keep handy and I start to write.

Dear Calippa
I really need you to help me think this one through.
I've told you before just how I feel about Max. But I'm
going to have to make a decision as to where we go from
here, and I think I've got three choices.

Number one. *Accept the situation just as it is:*
He's got a wife who's ill and who's unlikely ever to get
better. But because he's a decent man he won't
abandon her, and because they're both Catholics,
divorce is out of the question for them. I've lost Reuben
and I can't believe that I'll ever find anyone who can
take his place. So Max and I find comfort in each other.
I guess that to some people I'm just his mistress (I hate

that word!) or I'm no better than 'a kept woman' (I hate that phrase even more!). But it doesn't feel tawdry like that to me. There are times when I really believe that we've got something special between us. And there are other times when I wonder if I'm playing with fire.

Number two. *Try to force the issue:*
Tell him that if he wants to be with me – as he tells me he does – then he needs to decide one way or the other. Either he overcomes his scruples and divorces his wife or it's over between us. That puts the onus on him. He has to make the choice and I then have to live with the outcome. Not sure if I can do that, though.

Number three. *Listen to Juliette's advice:*
She tells me that a relationship with a married man who's twice my age and has a wife who's sick and almost permanently hospitalised is bound to end in tears. I should walk away before I waste any more of my life in a relationship that's doomed and before I get hurt any more than I need to.

Those are the choices as I see them. The problem is that without Max I think I'd be as lost and on my own as you were when we first met in Kendrew's Department Store.
I'm grateful that you're always here as a sounding board. But I wish you could actually give me an answer on this one.
Lori

I put the exercise book in its place in the drawer, turn off the light and go back to bed beside Max, trying not to wake him. But he instinctively reaches out to touch me and realises immediately that I must have been out of bed for some time.

'You're cold,' he says sleepily, turning over and wrapping himself around me. 'Where have you been? What on earth have you been doing out of bed in the middle of the night?'

I make the excuse that I'd decided to rewrap one of his presents before morning. It had been done in a hurry, I explain, and it didn't look as nice as I wanted it to or as he deserved. That satisfies his curiosity and he's about to go back to sleep, until I whisper to him that I want him to make love to me. It's a request with which he's more than ready to comply. What I don't tell him as he reaches out and pulls me to him is that my hunger for such physical intimacy arises more from a desperate loneliness and longing to be close to another human being than from the abandoned sexual desire that often brings us together. The sense of lostness that came over me when I was expressing my concerns and working out my options in my letter to Calippa Cumberland floods through my soul even as my body responds to his advances. And as passion subsides and our bodies separate, I'm listening not to Max's breathless protestations of love but to the concerned voice of Madge Timmins in my head, whispering, 'Just be careful, Lori, my dear. Just be careful.'

8
Christmas Eve 2001
People who'll help you imagine a better future...

If anyone had told me twelve months ago that I wouldn't just be spending Christmas with Madge Timmins but actually lodging with her, I would have laughed at such a ludicrous idea. But now, sitting with my feet up and drinking an after-dinner cup of coffee in Madge's front room – brought to me on a tray draped in an embroidered cloth by the lady of the house who's more than fifty years older than me! – I am more grateful than I can say for this place of refuge and for the company of the woman sitting opposite me.

Relaxing here in the safety and comfort of this home, I could almost believe that the last year has been just a bad dream. If only... If only it had all been just a nightmare from which I could have woken and then allowed it to slowly fade from my memory. Alas, it was all too real and will stay with me for a long time. I'm not sure if I'll ever completely get over what's happened, but I am feeling better than I dared to hope just a few short months ago.

It all began back in January when I went back to work at school after the Christmas break. I walked into the staffroom after lunch on the first day of term to be greeted by two male teachers humming the tune that had become all too familiar over the holiday period. The very same tune I'd played to Max on Christmas Eve, much to his annoyance – December's surprise chart topper, the theme music from a children's television cartoon about a builder and his friends.

At first, I didn't pay any particular attention to it. Eddie Johnson was a colleague in the English Department with whom I never felt I had anything in common other than our chosen profession. Ben Bolton was what I, quite unfairly, I'm sure, considered a typical PE teacher – more concerned about enlarging his muscles than expanding his mind and a bit raucous at staff get-togethers, though he'd always been friendly enough on the few occasions we'd spoken to each other. So I thought nothing more about it than that they were still in high spirits after the festive period and were attempting to ease themselves back into the routine of work. But when the same thing happened the following day, I began to suspect that something was afoot.

Before the end of the week, the humming had given way to singing. And the sniggering and glances in my direction when they reached the refrain and asked each other loudly if they could build it and responded even more raucously that yes they could made it clear that this performance was especially for my benefit.

I mentioned it to Juliette as we were walking home together on the Thursday afternoon, and I could tell immediately from her reaction that she was aware of what was happening.

'Hmm… *c'est pas gentil.* Not nice at all,' she responded with a grimace and a shake of her head. 'I was worried that something like that might happen. And I've picked up the gossip in the staffroom. I wasn't sure whether I should mention it to you. But word's obviously got around about you and Max. Someone saw you both at St Austen's on Christmas Eve, and whoever it was has obviously been talking about it. From what I can gather, Max isn't too popular with some folk on the staff…'

She hesitated as if she wasn't quite sure how to continue. But I pressed her to say what was on her mind, even though I had a sense of foreboding about what might come next.

'Well… Max did some work on the house of friends of Ben Bolton's parents four or five years ago. There was nothing wrong with the job. But according to Ben – and I have to say that Ben has a reputation for telling a good story – Max, who decided to do most of the work himself, made advances to their daughter when she was the only other person in the house. She was a few weeks short of her sixteenth birthday at the time and particularly vulnerable, having broken up with her boyfriend, whom she'd been going out with since they were both thirteen.'

We were passing the gate to the park at that moment and Juliette suggested that we should go in and sit on one of the benches before she went on with her story. I felt my stomach begin to tighten as I braced myself for what I was about to hear.

'Now, you need to know that I can't vouch for the accuracy of what Ben's been saying around the staffroom,' she said, as we settled ourselves on a bench far enough away from the path for our conversation not to be overheard, 'though he swears his story is true. He says Max got the girl pregnant. It all got covered up. Max paid for an abortion at a private clinic, didn't charge for the work he'd done on the house and paid the girl's parents a substantial sum of money to keep the whole thing quiet.'

I tried several times to respond. I wanted to protest that nobody with any sense would pay any attention to anything Ben Bolton said. I wanted to insist that I didn't believe a word of it. I wanted to tell Juliette that I was angry with her for even passing on such ridiculous nonsense to me. I wanted to stand up and scream that it simply wasn't true. But I couldn't find my voice. All I could do was cry. Tears of frustration at life for disappointing me again. Tears of anger at myself for being fool enough to trust another man. And tears of sheer hopelessness.

I'm still not sure how I got home that day. Juliette has told me that she walked all the way with me and stayed with me for an hour until she thought I was sufficiently composed to be left on my own. But I don't remember any of that. The first thing I do remember is waking up about five o'clock the next morning, still wearing my clothes and with a blinding headache and the worst pain in my stomach I've ever had.

I knew that there was no way I could go into school that day. I got undressed, stood under the shower for twenty minutes, wrapped myself in a towel for another ten minutes, and took the phone off the hook before crawling under the duvet again.

I was still in bed when I heard the sound of the key turning in the lock just after one o'clock in the afternoon.

'Helloooo! Anybody at home?' It was Max, who seemed to be trying a little too hard to sound cheerful. 'Just wanted to check that you're alright.'

Juliette had called him, he explained, telling him only that she was worried about me since I hadn't turned up for work and I wasn't answering the phone.

I wrapped my dressing gown round me and stumbled into the living room.

'Good grief, Lori,' he said coming towards me with his arms outstretched. 'You look terrible. What's happened?'

I slumped into the armchair and, between bouts of sobbing, I tumbled out the story that Juliette had relayed to me and demanded an answer to my question.

'Now, I want you to be honest with me. Did that really happen? And whatever you do, don't lie to me.'

He didn't respond immediately. For a second or two I thought I could see something like panic in his eyes. But he took a deep breath, resumed his usual confident expression and looked straight at me.

'Yes. I'm sorry,' he said slowly. 'It did happen. But what you've heard isn't the whole truth, by any means. It was a difficult time for me. Things were particularly bad with my wife's mental health. And I was under pressure with the business. I'd lost a couple of my best guys. That's why I was having to do so much of the work myself. Otherwise I'd never have been at the house.'

I could see he was anxious to emphasise that last point and I desperately wanted to believe him.

'So what happened? How did you end up making an underage girl pregnant?'

'Well, she threw herself at me – almost literally. She made all the running. And I honestly had no idea that she was only fifteen. She could easily have passed for a nineteen-year-old.' He looked at the floor. 'I'm a man, for goodness' sake, Lori. And I did tell you that there'd been a couple of times when I sought some comfort elsewhere. But I also told you that you and me – this is a completely different thing. This is more than just physical attraction. I love you.'

He crouched down in front of me and tried to take hold of my hands. But I got up quickly and pushed him away.

'You broke the law,' I objected. 'And then you covered it up. That was just wrong.'

'Oh, come on, Lori. Think about it.' There was a note of annoyance in his voice that he made no attempt to hide. 'What good would it have done anyone to report the matter? I would have had to defend myself in court, and that would have meant attacking her story and hurting her and her parents. It would have damaged my reputation and harmed my business prospects, and that could have cost half a dozen good tradesmen their jobs. And then there was my wife to think of. What the publicity would have done to her doesn't bear thinking about. No, sorting it out between ourselves was best thing – best for everybody concerned. And I'd have told you about it at some time. It just hasn't been the right time yet. I'm sorry that somebody's opened their big mouth and that you've had to find out about it like you have done.'

I desperately wanted to be convinced by his reasoning, and we tried to patch things up between us and carry on as before. I got my sympathetic GP to sign me off work for a month. But after I'd been back at school for less than two weeks, I knew I couldn't cope. I walked out halfway through a class on the second Friday afternoon and I've never been able to go back since then. Whether it was simply the stress of what had happened or whether the illness was just taking its inevitable course, I don't know. What I do know is that my endometriosis became even more debilitating. The bleeding became heavier and more unpleasant than ever, and I would wake often in the night with the bed damp from my sweating. Nausea and vomiting were frequent occurrences.

And things were never the same between Max and me. Sex ceased to be a pleasure and instead became an excruciatingly painful ordeal. Max tried to be sympathetic, but it became increasingly obvious that I had become involved with a man who had neither the depth of love to walk with me through what was happening nor the strength of character to cope with another unwell woman in his life.

There was no heated argument or tearful parting. He just got up and left one morning after a night in which, despite my symptoms being at their worst, we'd tried to make love. While we just about succeeded in some kind of unpleasant and unsatisfactory physical connection, we certainly did not 'make love'. Instead, it forced us to face the bleak truth that whatever love had existed between us before had completely gone from our relationship. Neither of us said anything other than a perfunctory goodbye and a vague promise to meet up later in the week. But we both knew that our relationship had come to an end and that we would never be together again. Indeed, apart from seeing him briefly on the opposite side of the street one rainy day, I've never even set eyes on him since.

Eventually, the worsening symptoms of my endometriosis forced me to go back to my GP, who was surprised to hear how the condition had progressed so dramatically. She immediately arranged for me to have an appointment with a specialist. I had expected to encounter a busy consultant with an efficient secretary who would remind me on arrival of his busy calendar and the need to be aware of the limited time at our disposal. Instead, a middle-aged matronly woman showed me into the somewhat untidy office of Mr Alastair McEuen, an elderly man with unruly, wavy white hair and a soft matching beard.

'Now, my dear,' he said in a soft breathy voice and a lilting accent that made me think of a trip I'd once made to the Scottish Highlands, 'take your time and tell me about your experience of endometriosis.'

He listened attentively and watched me closely as I spoke, lowering his head and taking his eyes off me only when he needed to write something on the notepad on the desk in front of him. I hesitated once or twice, unsure if I was talking too much or if he wanted to interrupt. But each time I paused, he smiled and indicated with a wave of his hand that I should continue. Only when I'd run out of things to say did he put down his pen and sit back in his chair.

'Thank you. That's very helpful to me. Though I have to say that yours is a story I've heard too often in the past and that I'm still hearing too often now.'

'I'm sorry,' I interjected a little nervously. 'You must get bored hearing the same thing over and over again.'

'Oh no… I don't mean that. And I'm certainly not bored, though I do sometimes find myself getting just a little angry. And I frequently find myself feeling very guilty too. There was a time when I didn't take your condition too seriously myself. Then, twenty-five years ago, my teenage daughter began having problems. Problems that she's had to live with ever since. That was the thing that began to change my attitude.' He ran his fingers through his shock of white hair and gave an apologetic smile. 'I was saying to one of my colleagues just the other day that if men suffered from endometriosis, we'd have put a lot more effort into discovering a cure, or at least finding a more effective treatment regime, years ago. But for too long we dismissed it as just "women's problems", and I'm sorry about that. It's certainly not a minor condition and it's certainly not a case of "the weaker sex" – another phrase I've grown to dislike – lacking the resolve to deal with it.'

He got up, walked round from behind his desk and pulled up a chair opposite me.

'I don't know if anyone has properly explained to you what's happening in your body. But let me try to do that as simply as I can. And stop me if you've heard all this before.' He spoke quietly and slowly, making me feel that talking to me was the most important thing he had to do that day. 'Every month, as you know, Mother Nature does her wonderful work. A woman's body goes through changes, and hormones are released that cause the lining of the womb to increase in preparation for a fertilised egg that will become an embryo and, if all goes well, grow into a healthy baby. But, if the egg isn't fertilised and pregnancy doesn't occur, this lining will break down and bleed. And the name we give to that, as you know all too well, is a woman's monthly period. So far, so good…'

Just at that moment the telephone on his desk rang and his manner changed immediately. He picked up the receiver and demanded to know who was calling. I felt a little sorry for his secretary when he instructed her brusquely to tell the hospital administrator that he was dealing with a patient and that was a far greater priority for him than attending yet another management and strategy meeting at which his presence was expected and his time would in all likelihood be wasted. He put the phone down with a long sigh of irritation.

'My apologies for that interruption.' He was once again the calm, soft-spoken physician giving all his attention to his patient. 'Now where was I? Oh yes… when a woman has endometriosis as you do, cells like those in the lining of the womb are found elsewhere in the body. We still don't really know why that happens. But each month these renegade cells react in the same way as those in the womb in response to the menstrual cycle. Just like them, they build up, then break down, and then start to bleed. And that's where the problem arises. Because, unlike the cells in the womb that leave the body naturally as a period, this blood has no way to escape, nowhere to go. And, in addition to heavy periods, this results in inflammation and pain and causes scar tissue to form. So something that should be natural and relatively trouble-free becomes a major problem. For reasons we don't always understand, things have gone awry. Life, I'm afraid, is sometimes like that…'

It was those last few words that got to me. His summing up of endometriosis was like a metaphor for my whole life. Everything was out of place and things had definitely gone awry. I tried with every bit of strength I possessed to keep a grip on my emotions, but they swept over me in an enormous crashing wave.

I've heard it said that when people are drowning, the whole of their life flashes in front of them. I've no idea if that's true. But I can vouch for the fact that such a thing can certainly happen when you're drowning in floods of tears. Every bitter memory was vividly present in that moment – my father's infidelity and subterfuge, Reuben's tragic and unexpected death, Max's weakness and disloyalty, my own stupidity in getting involved with a married man despite the concern of my friends, the mocking of teaching colleagues that had sapped my confidence and made me afraid to go back to school. And before I knew what I was doing, I heard myself telling the whole sorry saga to Mr McEuen while the tears streamed down my face. Several times I attempted to curb the torrent of words coming from my mouth, to make some kind of apology, to wipe my eyes. And each time he simply smiled and told me not to worry and not to stop.

He listened quietly and patiently until it was clear that I'd said everything I needed to say. Even then, he sat without speaking, leaving the room in complete silence for what seemed like a long time. When he did respond, he did so in a matter-of-fact manner that assured me he wasn't in the least embarrassed by my outpouring of emotion.

'Well, it was important for you to get that out. Thank you for trusting me enough to share it with me. And you can be sure of my professional confidentiality.'

He leaned over towards his desk, made some brief notes and told me that he'd arrange to see me again in a month. It was only then that I glanced at my watch and realised that what should have been a fifteen-minute appointment had stretched to almost three-quarters of an hour. I apologised for taking up so much of his time and stood up ready to leave. But he hadn't done with me yet.

'Before you go, Ms Bloom,' he said, as he walked over to open the door for me, 'there are some things I need to say to you. With regard to your endometriosis, I'm sorry that we don't have a cure. It's something you're going to have to live with. And there *will* be ways in which it will negatively impact your life. But that's not the whole story. There *are* treatments we can offer. We *are* learning ways to help you manage it, to alleviate the most unpleasant symptoms, to enable you to cope with it and still live a very full and worthwhile life. So it's by no means all doom and gloom. There really is light at the end of this tunnel.'

He reached out and gave me a firm handshake and a warm smile. But before he allowed me to leave, he had something more to say. Something that I hadn't expected.

'As for the other things you've shared with me, well, I hope you won't mind if I venture a little outside my area of professional expertise and offer you a bit of fatherly advice. There's no doctor who can cure the past, in the sense of making it all as if it had never happened. It's part of who you are and who you'll always be, just as much as your endometriosis is. And yes, it will shape your character in some ways, though that needn't just be for the worse. But it doesn't have to define you or to dictate your future. You *can* learn how to deal with it. And, just as there have been people who've hurt you, I hope and believe that you *will* meet people who'll want to help you. People who'll give you hope. People who'll help you imagine a better future.'

I walked along the corridor and out of the hospital. I felt my spirits lift even though nothing had really changed. I still had to live with endometriosis and I still had to deal with the hurts of the past. I knew in my heart of hearts that I didn't have the emotional strength to return to teaching. And I was growing increasingly ill at ease in the basement apartment that I'd once loved so much. What had been a haven now felt like a prison where I was haunted by bitter regrets and stalked by an ever-present guilt over my stupidity in allowing myself to be bought and owned by a man who'd never truly loved me.

It was, I was forced to acknowledge, a prison of my own making, but one from which I wanted to escape at the earliest opportunity. And Mr McEuen's words were like a shaft of light shining through the bars of a tiny window high up in the wall of the cell I had constructed for myself. And the kindly manner in which he had delivered his 'bit of fatherly advice' kindled in me the first faint stirrings of a hope that I might one day break out and walk free into a sunlit world.

It was only a week later that I answered a knock at my door, just before noon, to find Madge Timmins standing there with a bunch of flowers in her hand. She brushed aside my apologies for still being in my dressing gown at that hour of the day and pre-empted my hesitant invitation by telling me that she'd like to come in and talk to me. Before I realised what was happening, she'd taken charge of things and even managed to rustle up some lunch for me from the few basic groceries I had in my kitchen. And as I ate, she arranged the flowers in a vase and chatted to me about why she'd come. She'd heard rumours about what had happened, she'd made it her business to contact Juliette to find out the truth, and she had a proposal to make.

'Over the years I've often had someone lodging with me – you know, overseas students who were looking for somewhere to stay that they could afford, young folk who needed a home for a time, people who were going through a tough spell – that kind of thing. Sometimes they needed somewhere to stay just for a week or two and sometimes it's been longer than that. A couple of my guests were with me for more than a year.'

Having arranged the flowers to her satisfaction, she set them on the sideboard, sat down opposite me and came straight to the point.

'Juliette told me that you're feeling unsettled here in your apartment. Too many unhappy memories, she said. I can understand that. So why don't you come and stop with me for a little while? Just until you've sorted things out and you're ready to move on. I think you could do with some space to think and someone to look after you for a bit. Give you a little TLC. And I always enjoy the company of younger people. What do you think?'

I needed no second bidding. The next day, I paid the final month's rent on the apartment, mailed the keys back to Max's office and moved in with Madge. Juliette is storing some of my stuff in her attic, but Madge has insisted that I bring my old station waiting room clock that I've had since childhood and the sideboard that was my first purchase when I was furnishing the apartment. She says it's important that I have some familiar things around and feel at home for as long as I'm with her.

That was just over a month ago and I'm gradually beginning to feel more like myself. Hormone therapy has helped to ease the symptoms of my endometriosis a little, and I'm sure that Madge's unfussy care and the peacefulness of her home are having as much of a healing effect as anything else. Later this evening we'll go to the Christmas Eve service at St Austen's together. In fact, she's just suggested that I might want to assist her in her welcoming duties as the congregation arrives. To my surprise, I've agreed, though there's a question that I can't avoid asking her.

'Don't you think it'll look a bit odd to the regular attenders to have someone like me who's only ever turned up at Christmas greeting them as they enter?'

'Well, I don't know of anything in any church rulebook that demands a minimum number of visits before you're allowed to help or just take part in being nice to people.'

Judging from her chuckling, the thought of such a rulebook is amusing her greatly. 'For all I know, such a book must exist somewhere, but I've never read it and I certainly don't intend to. So you don't need to worry on that score.'

'But isn't that how you see the Bible? You know, God's rulebook? I remember there was a girl in my year at university who used to call it the Maker's Instructions.'

It suddenly occurs to me that I've blurted that out without thinking and I feel bad about it. Since I've been living here, Madge has treated me only with kindness, never once preaching at me or pressurising me to go to church with her. I know she takes her faith very seriously – praying and reading the Bible and going to church and doing all kinds of good deeds – but she's never once tried to force it on me. I immediately apologise for speaking out of turn. But Madge doesn't seem to be in the least offended by my comments.

'I know what you're saying, Lori. People do sometimes describe the Bible like that. I do understand what they're trying to say. And yes, it does contain rules, if you want to call them that. Forbidding us to lie or steal or murder, well, those actually seem pretty good rules to me. And, of course, there are the positive commands, like loving our neighbours as ourselves. The world would be a lot better if we all obeyed that one. But I don't read it like a rulebook. I mean, apart from anything else, rulebooks are pretty boring. It's not a description I like or one that I ever use.'

I've noticed this before with Madge. Whenever our conversations touch on any aspect of her faith, she never says more than she absolutely needs to in response to my questions. She never answers more than I ask or seems at all concerned to drive home her point. Whether this is a way of arousing my curiosity or something she's not even aware of, I've no idea. But it always has a strangely disconcerting effect on me. Part of me wants to leave the subject right there and move on, while another part – the part that usually wins – can't resist trying to find out what she's holding back, what she hasn't said. It happens again now.

'So, if it isn't a rulebook, then what is it?' I ask, knowing that I might hear more than I bargained for. 'It often seems to people like me who are not believers and who've never actually read the Bible at any depth that that's how Christians use it – to give you grounds for whatever position you take on some ethical issue, or to tell the rest of us what we're doing is wrong, or just to claim that you've got God on your side in the argument.'

As soon as I hear myself say those words, I feel annoyed with myself again and I want to apologise for being so unpleasant and argumentative to someone who's gone out of her way to be kind to me. But Madge appears to be quite unperturbed by what I've just said.

'Hmm… I'm not sure you're being entirely fair there, Lori. Mind you, I've got to admit that you're not being completely unfair either. We *do* fall into that trap sometimes. But personally, I think the biggest problem with using the Bible as a book of rigid rules like that is that it tends to make us confrontational. So we come up with arguments where everything is black and white, and we forget that ethical issues are sometimes really complex and that they involve people struggling to find their way through complicated situations rather dealing with black-and-white issues. And when I read the Gospel stories about Jesus, he always seems to be far more concerned about people and how to help them rather than just focusing on hard principles and how to apply them. In fact, that was his beef with the Pharisees, who specialised in doing just that.'

She pauses, takes off her glasses, huffs on them and gives them a polish with her apron, without taking her eyes off me for a second. This is something else I've noticed before in conversations with her. I suspect it's got little if anything to do with the need to clean her specs and a lot more to do with making you wait and ensuring that she's got your attention before she puts them back on and starts speaking again.

'You know, the older I get and the more I read the Bible, the more I see it as an invitation to imagine. Do you know what I mean by that?'

I confess that I don't and that even for someone like me with a degree in English and a love of literature, my few attempts to read the Bible have always proved to be hard going. I tell her that she's got a job on her hands persuading me of that between now and when we leave for the carol service at St Austen's.

'Oh yes, I'm glad you reminded me of the time,' she says, rubbing her hands on her apron and getting up. 'I know, when I get started in a conversation like this I could go on all night. That's what women of my age do. Yes, let's leave it and we can talk about it another time if you want.'

I realise immediately that I've played right into her hands with my comments. I've discovered since I've been living here that Madge conducts conversations like this with all the cunning of a chess master, letting you imagine that you're in control before she springs the trap. She'll say something that arouses your curiosity to the point at which you've just got to know where it is she's leading you. Then she'll smile sweetly, get up and get on with something completely unrelated, leaving you hanging there. You can try to ignore it and say nothing. But then you can't get it out of your mind, and you end up waking in the middle of the night wondering what it was she was going to say. Or, as I do now, you demand that she stays right where she is and finishes off what she was about to tell you. Which, of course, is exactly what she wants.

'Alright, since you insist. But just quickly, because time's going.' She says this with an expression of feigned innocence that would do justice to a Victorian portrait of a pious grandmother. 'Well, for a start, most of what you find in the Bible isn't rules and laws at all. It's stories and poems and prayers. That kind of thing. Then there are the letters that were sent to groups of people whose exact circumstances we don't know. There are even some strange visions whose precise meaning isn't at all easy to pin down. So all the way through, if you take the time to read it, your imagination is being engaged and stretched.'

She sits down again, pauses for a moment and nods her head, as if she's confirming to herself that she's absolutely convinced of the truth of what she's going to say.

'But it's more than that. Oh, I know it can be tough going at times when you're trying to read through it. But it's worth persisting because it's really one big, sweeping story about how the world was meant to be and about why it's in the state it's in. Above all, it's about the hope that the true order of things will be restored and love and peace will reign. Now, I'm the first to admit that when you look around you that takes a bit of believing. And sometimes you have to hang on to it despite all the evidence that seems to point in the opposite direction. And hanging on like that is what we usually call faith. But I think faith is at its heart an invitation to imagine. An invitation to imagine that the world can be transformed and that people can be changed, to imagine what or who might make that happen, and then to commit yourself to live for that. Hold on a minute while I look for something…'

My heart sinks when she leans over to the bookcase, pulls a leather-bound Bible off the shelf and thumbs through it until she finds the page she's looking for. I'm definitely not ready for this. Accompanying Madge to St Austen's and singing carols by candlelight is one thing. That *does* appeal to my imagination. But listening to a lengthy reading in a language that I remember one of my university lecturers telling us was already archaic by the time of Shakespeare – well, that's more than I can take on Christmas Eve. Madge, however, has noticed my discomfort.

'Don't worry, Lori,' she says with a chuckle. 'I'm not going to preach you a sermon. I'm just checking for one short sentence. I want to get it exactly right because it gets to the heart of what I'm trying to tell you. Here it is: Let me read it to you: "Now faith is being sure of what we hope for, being convinced of what we do not see." Now what is that, if it's not a description of imagination – being sure of what you hope for and being certain of what you can't see? Imagining what the world *could* be like, *should* be like, *will* be like if love and goodness were to lie at the very heart of things.'

She slides the Bible back into its place on the shelf and looks at me through narrowed eyes.

'Now, that's what I'm staking everything on. And that's what I've tried to live my life for. Though I should admit that I've done that very imperfectly and made more than a few mistakes along the way. You must make up your mind for yourself. Is it just the wishful thinking of a woman who's getting near the end of her life and wants to believe everything will turn out alright? Or has this old woman stumbled across the thing that makes sense of life?'

Madge glances at the clock on the wall, gets to her feet and starts to undo her apron. She tells me with a chuckle that what we certainly both can agree on is that if we don't get a move on, the impatient early comers, intent on getting the best seats in the house, will be locked out in the cold and in danger of losing the Christmas spirit.

By half past ten, she and I have taken our places in the draughty porch of St Austen's, where we hand out the customary carol sheets and candles in little paper cups and smile sweetly at the Christmas Eve congregation as they file into the church.

Whether it was the conversation about imagination earlier in the evening that did it, I don't know. But the service that evening has a magical quality I haven't experienced previously. After several years of trying to give it a more contemporary feel, the vicar has decided to revert to something much more traditional and to follow the structure of the Nine Lessons and Carols. The familiar readings – familiar even to someone like me who knows little of the Bible – seem to penetrate my consciousness at a level far deeper than mere understanding; the sound of the hymns and carols echoing through the building have a strangely haunting quality; the sight of the crudely constructed crib in front of the altar and surrounded by straw scattered across the floor makes me want to cry; and the moment when the lights are dimmed and the place is illuminated only by two hundred candles held aloft makes my heart beat a little faster.

As we walk home together, our breath making clouds that appear for a moment in the cold night air before vanishing from sight, we chat about the service and agree that it was an experience we will treasure. In my enthusiasm, I tell Madge that no Christmas Eve has made such an impression on me since that late afternoon in Kendrew's Department Store in Bristol on the 24th of December a quarter of a century earlier. I tell her about Calippa Cumberland.

As I expected, she's amused and charmed by the name that I was convinced I'd heard coming over the public address system. But to my surprise, she's so intrigued by my story that she insists I repeat it to her several times. And as I do so, I hear myself confiding to her that the little lost girl with the curly blonde hair has become my imaginary friend. A friend not just through childhood years, but a friend in whom I still confide in my almost daily journal.

As soon as the words are out of my mouth, I regret what I've just done. Even to someone as understanding as

Madge, it must sound like the confession of a person who's lost touch with reality. Imagination is one thing, but what sane and normal person would continue to write letters to someone they've never actually seen and whose proper name they don't even know?

But Madge is unperturbable as ever and even more curious. She asks me if I have any idea why the experience made such a lasting impression on me. Why the little lost girl with the curly blonde hair has become part of my life.

'I don't know. Oddly enough, it's not a question I've ever asked myself.' I take a moment to think, unsure how to explain it, even to myself. 'Maybe... maybe it's because Calippa Cumberland is a kind of kindred spirit. Or maybe, more accurately, she's become some sort of *alter ego*. Maybe it's because I think I know how she must have felt. Or maybe it's because I think she might be the only person I've encountered who might understand how *I* feel. You know... a little bit lost in a big world...'

My words peter out and I wonder if I'm making any sense at all or just talking pretentious nonsense. I half expect Madge to reply, perhaps even to take advantage of the situation and deliver a brief homily on the topic of my 'spiritual condition'. But she says only 'Uh-huh' and gives the slightest nod of her head. Then she slips her hand into mine and squeezes it very gently. And as we walk home hand in hand, I become aware of the frosty night air stinging my cheeks. I'm beginning to cry.

I don't reach into my coat pocket for a tissue and I don't try to stop the tears running down my face. I just want to be allowed to cry. I need to cry. I need to cry for all that's been lost. I'm crying for that little lost girl who, in my imagination, is still wandering alone through Kendrew's Department Store. I'm crying for my father who was lost to me years ago in his pathetic world of make-believe and sham relationships. I'm crying for my mother who lost her husband and almost lost her sanity and self-respect in that period of her life when alcohol was her only comfort. I'm crying for Reuben Hodgson who lost his life in the cold, dark waters of Wythmere. And I'm crying for me, Lori Bloom, a woman just short of her thirties who's already lost so much and who's just owned up to someone that she feels lost in the world.

We keep on walking, I keep on crying, and Madge just keeps holding my hand and saying 'Uh-huh' whenever my tears flow a little more readily. By the time we reach home, I'm quite exhausted and I'm ready to head straight to bed. Madge, however, decides we both need a hot drink before we retire for the night. A cup of hot chocolate, she's told me more than once, is the most comforting thing in the world after you've had a proper cry and the best thing for ensuring that you get a good night's sleep.

Neither of us speaks until we've drained the last dregs from our cups. I have just enough energy to say goodnight, but Madge has one last thing to say.

'God bless you, my child. You've had some tough times and there may be a few more to come. But you'll be alright. And don't worry about writing letters to Miss Cumberland. If it helps you to work things out, that's OK. And who knows, you might even find her one day.' She gives another of her little chuckles. 'Anyhow, I'm the last person to think you're crazy. Goodness me, every night before I sleep I have a conversation with someone I can't see, who many people tell me is a figment of my imagination and whose existence I can't prove. So you're in good company here.'

As soon as I get into my room, I get undressed and crawl into bed. There's one last thing I have to do before I can allow myself to fall asleep. So I take the pencil and the exercise book from my sideboard and prop the pillows behind my back so that I can sit up and write. The first two words are easy enough, the same as always:

Dear Calippa

Then I pause and try to think how I can sum up the day. There's so much I could say. So much I want to say. But I feel the pencil slipping out of my hand and I know I'm not going to manage to write another word. I rearrange the pillows and lie down. And in less than a minute. I'm sound asleep.

9
Christmas Eve 2006
The man you're about to meet is a different person...

The sign in the window says that the premises do not open until six o'clock in the evening on Christmas Eve. But in response to my knocking the door is opened just a few inches, and after a few brief, whispered questions to ascertain my identity, I'm admitted by a man who tells me he's the landlord. I step out of the bright light and the bracing breeze of the late morning into the stillness and comparative gloom of The Sailor's Rest, still unsure why I've allowed myself to be persuaded to be here today.

Everything feels unreal, like a scene from a second-rate spy thriller in which actors who are unsure of their lines will play out their roles against an unconvincing backdrop. Everything about the olde-worlde interior I've just entered is designed to persuade me that I'm in a traditional English pub that has stood on this same spot since the sixteenth century, unravaged by the passing of time. Everything, that is, except for the fact that it's on the ground floor of a fifteen-storey building overlooking the marina and was constructed at the beginning of the new millennium as part of the local council's drive to persuade visitors to the West Country to travel the ten miles from Bristol and discover for themselves the delights of Avonhead's riverside pleasures. This is a place where things are not as they seem at first glance.

That, however, makes it an appropriate setting for what is about to happen in the seclusion of this mock-Tudor tavern. To a casual observer it might appear to be a typical gathering of old friends or family members meeting in the conducive atmosphere of a comfortable pub for a happy reunion. An opportunity to swap oft-repeated tales of growing up and growing into adulthood together, entirely unconcerned about who might overhear their reminiscences or be disturbed by their uproarious laughter. But so intent are the members of this group on securing the strictest privacy for their meeting that they have booked the entire premises right through until the afternoon. And I wonder again why I have agreed to be part of this clandestine gathering whose outcome is so unpredictable.

I make my way across the otherwise empty room to a round table at which two other people are already seated, awaiting my arrival – a man and a woman, both, like me, in their mid-thirties. The man comes towards me with his hand outstretched.

'Good morning. You must be Lori. Thanks for coming. I'm Greg, Greg Sanderson. And this is my half-sister…' He pauses, amused by what he's just said, and then adds, 'Well, she's you're half-sister too, for that matter – Norah Erdington.'

It startles me when I see his face up close. He has the same colouring as me and he looks exactly like I remember my father the last time I saw him. The same thick, black, wavy hair, the same deep-blue eyes, the same Hollywood matinee-idol looks that make me think of a time long gone. And his voice is no less arresting. It's immediately obvious when he speaks that he moves in the kinds of circles where it's important to communicate formally and precisely, though there are still unmistakable traces of his Geordie roots. This is a man who was raised and still lives in Newcastle. But, for all that, the timbre of his voice is such that I can hear my father speaking again. The resemblance is so striking that I feel as if I've been transported back to my teenage years and I struggle to find the words to respond to his greeting. He shrugs and smiles in a manner that tells me this isn't the first time he's had this kind of reaction.

'I know exactly what you're thinking. I've seen that expression before. I *do* look like our father. I guess I'm very fortunate to have inherited his good looks.'

My instinct is to reply that I hope that's all that's been bequeathed to him from his father – his appearance and not his character. But before I can yield to that impulse, the woman who's been introduced as my half-sister gets up and shakes my hand. Unlike Greg and me, she's fair-skinned and has light-brown hair. I guess that must come from her mother, and that fleeting thought stops me in my tracks and makes me realise again just how odd this whole thing is. Three of us, related by blood, with the same father but different mothers, and all three of us blissfully unaware of each other's existence for so much of our lives.

And now here we are, all three of us in the same place for the first time, all three of us waiting nervously for the arrival of the man without whose bizarre lifestyle we wouldn't be alive.

'And I think I know how you must be feeling right now, Lori.' Norah Erdington's voice breaks into my thoughts. 'It took a lot of persuasion from Greg to get me here too. And I'm still nervous about what's going to happen. But in the end I thought it was the right thing to do. If only for my mother who, despite everything, still pines for what she calls the best days of her life. Greg pulled off the motorway at Birmingham and picked me up at one of the services on the way here earlier this morning. So he's had time to bring me up to date with the latest twist in the story. But I think he needs to tell you what's he's told me before our father gets here.'

All I know is what Greg Sanderson told me a week ago in a phone call that came out of the blue. Until 1986, when his father's true identity had been exposed and the shocking truth of his duplicitous behaviour had emerged, Bert Sanderson – that was the name he'd used with this particular branch of his 'family' – had been his hero. He'd longed for his return every day during his long absences, and his visits 'home', all too brief though they were, had been the highlights of Greg's childhood. And whereas my anger at Bart Bloom's behaviour had meant that I'd tried to erase every vestige of his memory from my mind, he'd thought about his father every day. Even the disappointment and hurt that his conduct had caused could not overcome the love and admiration the boy still felt. And now that he was married with two children of his own, he'd become increasingly anxious that his children should know their grandfather. The success of his importing business had provided him with the kind of financial security and disposable income that had allowed him to invest considerable funds in employing a private investigation agency who'd succeeded not only in tracing his father's whereabouts, but also in finding out who his half-siblings were and where they were living.

Towards the end of that telephone call, Greg told me that our father had agreed to meet him in The Sailor's Rest by the marina in Avonshead, but only on one condition: that his two other children, Norah and me, could be persuaded to attend. At first, I'd refused point-blank, telling him that I never wanted to see the man again. In the end, however, although I don't quite understand why, I'd yielded to his pleading. Now Norah's reference to another twist in the story is making me regret my decision. Surely Bart Bloom, or Bert Sanderson, or whatever he called himself when he was with Norah's mother, hasn't been up to his old tricks again!

'So what have you told Norah that you haven't yet told me?' I ask, looking at Greg accusingly. 'It wouldn't take much for me just to walk out the door if I hear something I don't like. And I don't want you to think that I'm happy to be part of a welcoming party for a returning hero.'

'He's certainly not that. Far from it. So you can relax on that score. He'll be here in ten minutes or so. Let's sit down and I'll tell you what I learned just a couple of days ago.'

Somewhat grudgingly, I take my place at the table, opposite my half-sister, to hear what Greg has to say.

'It's just over two months since I first got in touch with him. I must have spoken to him seven or eight times on the phone and I could sense from those conversations that he wasn't in a good place. Neither literally nor emotionally. He's been living in some fairly rundown rental accommodation just outside Southampton. The two men from among his old criminal associates from whom the police considered him to be most at risk both died some years ago. But even though he's been safe from any threat from that quarter for quite a while, he's still been living under the name of Brian Bridges.'

I can't resist interjecting that, confusing as this array of names is for us, it should be easy enough for a man who's been able to come up with new names and new identities with some ease whenever it's suited his purposes.

'You may be right,' Greg replies with a rueful expression. 'But you need to know that the man you're about to meet is a different person from who he was the last time any of us saw him. And the latest bit of news I have from him – and I'm as sure as I can be that this isn't another of his con-tricks or a play for sympathy – is that he's been diagnosed with terminal lung cancer and that he only has a matter of months to live. I can certainly vouch for the fact that, from what I heard over the phone, he's got a very unhealthy-sounding hacking cough. That's all I can tell you. But I thought it best that you prepare yourself for how he might look.'

I'm struck with a sudden pang of guilt for what I said a minute or two ago and I wonder whether I should apologise. But Greg glances at his watch, pushes his chair back from the table and stands up.

'You need to excuse me. Somebody he knows is driving him up from Southampton and dropping him off outside and I promised I'd be waiting for him at the door when he gets here.'

When we're left on our own, Norah Erdington and I look at each other across the table. I'm guessing that, just like me, she's trying to think of something to say that won't be an inane cliché. But when I do manage to speak, that's exactly what my words amount to.

'Well, I guess I should say that despite the circumstances, it's very nice to meet you, Norah.'

No sooner is the tired old platitude out of my mouth than the two of us, confronted by the oddness of the situation in which we find ourselves and embarrassed by the banality of my greeting, begin to giggle uncontrollably.

We're still giggling like two nervous schoolgirls when we hear the sound of the door opening on the opposite side of the room, and Greg returns with my father walking slowly alongside him. He's a full six inches shorter than his son, who looks exactly as I remember my father looking at a similar age. For a moment, the two figures are silhouetted in the light flooding through the open door. It is an image that's visible for only a few seconds before the door closes behind them, shutting out the sunlight. But it will remain etched on my memory for ever. It's as if the laws of time have been suspended and I am being allowed a vision of my father in his prime again – tall, handsome, imposing – standing alongside the stooped and shrunken figure he has become in the two decades since I last saw him. The anger that has gnawed at my soul for so long over his treatment of my mother and me and the irritation I've been feeling all morning at having to make this trip from London on Christmas Eve are swept away by a rush of sympathy for what time and sickness have done to him.

He walks slowly and a little unsteadily across the room. I don't know what the protocol is for a meeting like this. Should Norah and I stand? Should we embrace him? Or do we keep our distance, physically and emotionally, like unbiased jurors in a courtroom, reserving judgement until we hear what the accused has to say in his defence? I can see that he's as uncertain about what to do next as we are – unsure how much further he should come towards us, unsure whether to smile at us or to lower his head and avert his gaze.

It breaks my heart to see his diffidence and hesitancy and to remember that this was once the larger-than-life figure who could fill a room with his presence the moment he walked in the door. For years I've savoured the fact that justice was done and that he was incarcerated. But this looks like a human being who has not only been subjected to punishment but who has also been brought to the brink of destruction.

He's wearing a dark suit with what would once have been a white shirt and a wide tie displaying the kind of brash pattern that went out of fashion years ago. He even has a red silk handkerchief tucked in his top pocket, just as I remember him doing when I was a child. It's clear that he's made an effort to dress for the occasion. But his efforts cannot disguise the sad truth. His clothes are worn and shabby and he looks exhausted, tired to the bone and utterly weary of life. Whatever wrongs he has done, it's plain to see that he is paying a terrible price.

Greg helps him into one of the chairs around the table and releases the tension by joking that since we're the only people in the place, we must have made a bad choice of restaurant. As if on cue, just in case anyone took that comment seriously, a waiter comes discreetly into the room with coffee and tells us that lunch will be at half past one.

'I think you said that you wanted time to talk together before we serve your meal,' he says, as he sets out the cups. 'So that'll give you good time for your conversation. And I'll make sure that you're not disturbed for the next hour and a half.'

As soon as we're on our own again and coffee has been poured, Greg outlines briefly how he managed to track his father down and tells us of their initial tentative contact, first by letter and then, a few weeks later, over the phone.

'Those conversations,' he continues, 'brought me to the place where I believe that the time is ripe for us to see if we can begin to move towards some kind of reconciliation. I'm not sure that any of our mothers is ready for a meeting like this. But we're siblings and, apart from anything else, I think it's important for us to get to know each other. And when I discovered that our father is not in the best of health and was keen to meet with the three of us urgently, I decided to take the plunge and ask if you'd come today. I know he wants to speak to us. So I'll stop talking and let him get on with it.'

I've been trying to listen attentively to what Greg's been saying, but I'm struggling to get my head around the scene that's playing out before me. Is this really happening? Am I really sitting in the same room as my brother and sister whom I've never met and my father whom I haven't seen for twenty years? My sense of disbelief only increases as my father begins to speak.

'I don't know how you're all feeling right now...' His breathing is rapid and shallow, his words come slowly and his voice is barely more than a whisper. 'But I can tell you that I'm at least as nervous about this meeting as you must be. My emotions are all mixed up and I'm unsure of what to say first.'

He pauses for a moment and wipes his mouth with the red silk handkerchief he pulls from his jacket pocket. A vein on the side of his forehead is pulsing and his hands are trembling. He tries several times to tuck the handkerchief back into his pocket but manages only to get it halfway in before he starts speaking again. The sight of it hanging untidily down the front of his jacket and glistening with flecks of saliva fills me with a sadness so deep that it physically pains me.

'I know I need to apologise to you all for what I did. I've had a long time to reflect on how I behaved, and I still can't fully understand why I did what I did myself. The nearest I can get to any kind of explanation is that deep down I didn't think much of myself. People used to tell me I was good-looking when I was younger...' He pauses mid-sentence and gives a hoarse, cynical laugh at the memory. 'That's a joke when you look at me now. And I never really believed that it was true back then. So I had to keep proving it to myself. Proving that I was attractive to women. Proving that I was a *real* man, that I could father children. I found it hard to cope with ordinary everyday reality. At first, I just used to imagine myself living with another woman. Then I had to prove that to myself by actually living with another woman, having another child.

'All the other stuff – the stuff that got me into trouble with the law – wasn't that much different. I remember being told that I had movie-star looks. Maybe I had, though they're definitely long gone. Certainly I had a movie-star way of looking at life. I wanted to be like a character from one of the gangster films I loved. In fact, I wanted to have a starring role. I never really meant any harm. But it was pathetic. *I'm* pathetic and I'm sorry about all of it.'

He slumps back in his chair, exhausted by the effort of admitting the harsh truth. It must have been an enormous effort for a man who'd engaged in fantasy for so much of his life. Greg offers to refill his cup and he readily agrees.

None of us knows how to respond to what he's just said. We know that what we're hearing is nothing less than a confession of a wasted life from a man whose days are short. And it is both indescribably sad and unnervingly sacred to witness such a moment of contrition. He grasps his cup in both hands and sips the warm coffee gratefully, though he spills as much as he manages to drink. The caffeine seems to revive his flagging energy a little. But his hands still shake uncontrollably and the cup rattles against the saucer as he puts it down and prepares himself to continue.

In the silence that follows, the relentless rhythm of his laboured breathing has an unsettling effect on me. Of course, listening to anyone who has trouble getting their breath is in itself an unpleasant experience. But it's not just that that's disturbing me. At first, I can't understand why it's troubling me so much. Then it comes to me with a suddenness that shocks me. The rhythm of his breathing moves at the same pace as the solemn ticking of the old station waiting room clock that I have kept with me wherever I have lived across the years, never quite able to comprehend the fascination such things hold for me. But now I think I know. In fact, I think deep down I've probably known it since childhood. Known it even before Uncle Rob gave me the clock, known it even before my mother bought me my first wonderfully gaudy children's watch on that Christmas Eve in Kendrew's Department Store. Known it from the moment I learned to tell the time. I think I've really known all my life that the steady ticking of the seconds and the almost imperceptible moving of the hands – enthralling as they are to people with a mind like mine – are an inescapable reminder that time never stops, that day always moves into night, that each season gives way to another, that everything passes, and that ultimately every life will end. And now I am watching and listening as my own father, the man from whom my own life came, clears away the detritus of the years and readies himself for the end that is almost close enough for him to touch.

He forces himself to sit up straight in his chair, looks at each one of us in turn – first at me, then at Norah, then at Greg – and begins to speak again.

'Yes. I am sorry about all that. More sorry than I can say. And I've spent the last twenty years with a regret so bitter that I can almost taste it. But you need to know this.

I'm not sorry about fathering you three. I wish the circumstances had been different. But when I've gone, at least I know I'll have left something good behind. I know you three will still be here. The one thing I was able to keep from my old life was a handful of people in my old stamping grounds that I could still trust, though even with them I never risked giving away my whereabouts. I'd phone from callboxes in different towns and ask them to check up on how you were doing. And always they'd tell me you were doing well, growing up to be normal, decent people, despite the genes you'd inherited from me...'

A fit of coughing stops him from going any further and he pulls the red silk handkerchief out of his jacket pocket again and wipes his mouth. This time he doesn't try to fit it back in his pocket but crumples it up and tries to hold it in his right hand. The effort seems to make his hand tremble even more and the handkerchief slips from his grip and falls onto the table in front of him. It makes me think of the picture of the surrendered flag of a defeated and demoralised army that I once saw in a book. Bart Bloom may be both of those things – demoralised and defeated – but he isn't finished speaking yet.

'I'd apologise for that demonstration of how bad my health is,' he says, his voice still hoarse from the coughing fit. 'But I'd be apologising to people all day long and every day if I did that. But there is something else I need to tell you. I long ago promised myself that I'd never try to contact any of you. I've done enough damage to your lives as it is. But when Greg found out where I was and got in touch and asked to meet me, well, I couldn't let this opportunity pass. If I was going to meet with him then I wanted to meet with the three of you, just this once. And you certainly don't have to worry about me interrupting your lives and trying to make this an annual event. If this Christmas is to be my last, as the doctors are telling me, then I wanted to make it something special. Give myself a bit of a treat. That's why I asked Greg if he could arrange this meeting for Christmas Eve. A bit selfish of me, I know. But I hoped you'd understand. I'm sure I don't look great to you. But I can't tell you how good you three look to me.'

He sits back with the expression of a man who's completed a challenging mission and who can now take some rest. His eyes close and I wonder if he's actually fallen asleep, exhausted by the effort of delivering the speech he came to make.

I glance at Greg and Norah, unsure what to do next. But his eyes open slowly again and he looks at us. It is a look that is the perfect picture of mixed emotions, full of longing and regret and pride and gratitude. I can bear the silence no longer and I start to speak before I know what I'm going to say. But I know that whatever it is I have to say it.

'Well, Dad...' The word takes me by surprise. It's so long since I used it of my father that it sounds strange to me. But now that I've said it, I don't want to change it or withdraw it, and I say it again. 'Well, Dad, we all wish things could have been different. For everybody's sake. But they are what they are. And you are who you are. And we are who we are. I can't speak for the others, but I'm glad that you decided you wanted to meet us. And I'm glad that I overcame my reluctance and came today.'

I can hear Greg and Norah muttering their agreement and I decide to keep going and see where my words lead me.

'If we've only got limited time, then I think we should make the best of it. So I want to propose that we agree to meet again as soon as possible.'

It's a proposal that carries the judgement of the others, including my father, and the atmosphere in the room lightens noticeably as we fix on a date in the middle of January for another meeting. The enthusiasm is such that Norah and I agree to Greg's suggestion that the three of us should each talk to our mothers and invite them to join us when we meet again. Maybe, he says, time will have healed the hurts sufficiently for them to forgive. Or, at least, they might recognise our desire to acknowledge that, however odd the circumstances might be, we are siblings. An odd kind of family, but family all the same.

My father is hesitant about this, fearful of what their response is likely to be. But in the end he's persuaded because we believe it to be worth asking them and because he knows better than anyone else that time may not allow for a third meeting.

Lunch turns into an unexpected but unforgettable celebration. Like all the best meals, the food, good though it is, gives place in importance to the conversation. We remember the times when we would wait impatiently – in Bristol or Newcastle or Birmingham – for the man all three of us called Daddy to pull up in his sports car with the tyres screeching, ease himself out of the driver's seat, stretch himself and shake the stiffness out of his legs, sling his bag over his shoulder and come striding towards the house. We tell stories – all of them remarkably similar – of the presents he would bring and the games we would play with him, of being swung around the room as he held us by an arm and a leg, of boasting to classmates and friends that we had the best daddy in the world, even though his business kept him away for long weeks at a time as he 'earned the pennies' – it seems we all used those same words as children – that allowed us to live so well.

Recalling that familiar phrase from childhood reminds me that this man is far from being a storybook hero. This is a man who 'earned the pennies' by illegal activities. This is a man whose 'business' was not the respectable enterprise our neighbours assumed it to be. And we are the children of a convicted criminal who escaped a heavier sentence only by 'grassing' on his former associates. And yet, as I look at him across the table – old beyond his years, his body ravaged as a consequence of seeking solace in heavy drinking and what has clearly been an addiction to cigarettes – I know that he's paid a terrible price. He used his vivid imagination to invent for himself multiple identities and create for himself three different families. As a consequence, he has spent the last twenty years rejected by those whom, in his own strange way, he loved, trapped in an identity that has been forced on him. That must have been a far greater punishment than the years he spent in prison. And I no longer feel either anger or shame for his past. Only a deep and bitter sorrow for what he has become and for the ending that is so near.

When lunch is over and we're saying our goodbyes to each other, my father tells us that the acquaintance who drove him up from Southampton has had to go straight back and that he will need to get to Bristol Temple Meads station to catch a train home. I know my way around Bristol better than the others and I immediately volunteer to drive him there in my car, grateful for the opportunity to have some time to talk to him alone. As we walk slowly to the car park he explains his reason for suggesting to Greg that we should have our meeting somewhere near to Bristol.

'I thought it'd be a good chance to have a quick drive into the city on the way home, see some of my old haunts, maybe even have a quick look at the house on Morley Road. But that'll have to wait for another time.'

'Well, we can still do it,' I respond with an eagerness that surprises me for a moment, before I realise what's lurking at the back of my mind and prompting my readiness to be so helpful. *There probably won't be another time*. So I strike while the iron is hot. 'Yes, let's do it. I'd like to see the old place again too.'

Forty minutes later we're driving down Newman Hill. I slow down and pull into the side of the road, about twenty yards from the junction where we can see number 17 Morley Road right in front of us. In the fading light of the late afternoon the Bath stone walls seem to have lost something of their glow that I remember so fondly from childhood. But the high retaining wall protecting the garden is still there, and the place still has that imposing air of permanence and stability. The tall bay windows still look out on the world like the watchful gaze of a guardian angel.

I turn off the ignition and neither of us speaks for a full minute. I look at my father and see regret etched deeply on his face. It threatens to break my heart.

'Are you alright, Dad?' I ask, putting my hand gently on his arm. 'Do you want to get out? I could knock on the door and ask whoever lives there now if we could maybe step inside for a moment.'

'No, don't do that.' He gives me a tired smile and shakes his head. 'No, that'd be too much for me. It'd be like trying to go back and I know I can't do that. No, I'm just grateful to see it. A chance to remember how good things were and realise what a fool I was. But you'd better get me to the station or we'll miss that train.'

I'm just putting the car into first gear and thinking about the quickest way to the station when I stop and turn the ignition off.

'Dad, what will you be doing when you get back to Southampton? How will you be spending Christmas Day? You won't be on your own, will you?'

'Oh, you don't need to worry about me. I've got used to my own company. And there's a church along the road from the block of flats I'm in. They do Christmas lunch for folk like me. So I'll probably go there.'

He says it in such a matter-of-fact way, without a hint of self-pity in his voice, which somehow makes it all the harder to hear. For the second time in an hour, I act on instinct without giving any real thought to what I'm saying.

'Well, if you've got nothing special to go back to Southampton for, why don't you come and spend Christmas with me in London? I'm sure my friend Madge can find room for you. There's always a crowd at her house on Christmas Day. The spare room's empty at the moment. I'll give her a call and just make sure.'

At first, he's reluctant to accept the invitation. He's out of practice being with other people, he says. He'll feel embarrassed and awkward. And, apart from all that, he hasn't got any other clothes with him. He's grateful to me for thinking about him, but it's best if I just take him to the station. So I change tactics and approach it from another angle.

'Dad, I'm not trying to do you a favour. The truth is I want you to do this for me. You know how I loved it when I was a kid and you'd always turn up on Christmas Day. What you don't know is how much I've missed it since you were... well, you know what happened. My childhood ended abruptly then. So I think you owe me this one. It's me who's asking for a favour.'

That does it. A quick call to Madge, a mad dash to a menswear store in a retail park on the outskirts of the city to buy some items of clothing for my father, and by half past five we're leaving the M32, joining the M4 and heading for London. For the first thirty miles I tell him about my life over the last few years: my broken relationship with Max, though I decide that it's better to leave out the small but significant detail that he was a married man; how I moved in with Madge as a temporary measure five years ago and have never left; and about my unexpected change of career from teaching to becoming a researcher and occasional presenter at a north London independent radio station. He's genuinely interested and tries hard to listen, but when I see that he's struggling to stay awake, I cut short my mini autobiography and allow him to rest.

When I'm sure that he's asleep, I turn the radio on quietly and set it to a station where I know there'll be non-stop music to keep me alert. The first track I hear is a song by Take That. Boy bands are not normally my thing, but this song has deservedly become yet another seasonal surprise chart-topper. It's a long way from the usual pop hits extolling the bliss of adolescent love. The surprisingly mature lyrics are a plea for others to have patience with us as we seek healing from hurt and try to find a way to start all over again. I sing along under my breath, thinking what a strange and yet oddly appropriate song it is for us on this Christmas Eve.

I glance at the man sitting alongside me, now deep in sleep. With his head lolling back and his mouth hanging open, he looks much older than his years and utterly worn out by life. I find myself praying that there will be time for him to find healing for his hurts. I know, however, that it is too late for him to start again. That seems to happen more in the lyrics of popular songs than in the lives of people like my father.

It's almost nine o'clock when we reach the house just off the Holloway Road that's become home for me and where I've found a measure of healing and the strength to start again. I open the door to the sound of carols on the radio and the aroma of baking coming from the kitchen where Madge has obviously been busy making sure the preparations for tomorrow are complete before she leaves to fulfil her customary duty of welcoming the Christmas Eve congregation to St Austen's. As we step into the hallway, she appears, wiping her hands on her apron and waiting to greet us.

'Now, you must be Lori's dad,' she says, smiling at my father. 'She talks about you a lot, so I feel like I know you already. I'm so glad that you can spend Christmas here with your daughter. The spare room is all ready for you. I think you'll be quite comfortable.'

She ushers us into the kitchen where there is a place set on either side of the table. She brings the kettle to the boil and eases the cling film from the plateful of sandwiches it's been covering.

'Sorry I can't do something more elaborate for you at the moment. But I need to head out in half an hour. And Lori, don't worry about coming with me tonight. You've both had a long day. And don't sit up and wait for me coming in.'

I feel sorry about missing what's become a Christmas ritual that I look forward to every year. But I know she's right and that it will definitely be too tiring for my father. But he shakes his head, looks at me and then at Madge.

'No. That's very thoughtful of you. But you know, I'd really like to come, if you don't mind. I am a bit tired, but I'll sleep all the better tonight. I haven't been to a carol service since I was a kid at school. I'd really like to go to one with my daughter while I can.'

There's just time for him to wash and change into the clothes we bought in the afternoon before we set off. From somewhere, Madge rustles up a warm coat that's just the right size for him, and the three of us set off, arm in arm, across the pavement to make the short walk to St Austen's.

It turns into an evening I will never forget. We fetch him a chair beside me in the entrance porch where he can rest while I give out the carol sheets and candles to the arriving worshippers. The look on his face is enough to tell me that he's grateful for this opportunity and as proud of me as he would be if I were presenting gifts to royalty. And when the service begins and we've made our way to the pew at the back of the church, he struggles his way through the carols. I'm aware of one or two disapproving glances in our direction. Undoubtedly for some of the people around us it's probably a less-than-melodious sound. For me, however, it's music to my ears.

And when we've got home again and I've made sure that my father is asleep, I go to my room and take out the blue exercise book from the top of the pile and one of the pencils from the cup that sits on the old sideboard. I'm just about to write the words I've written so often over the years:

Dear Calippa...

Then I think better of it and close the book. I undress, turn off the light, get into bed and whisper very quietly, 'Calippa Cumberland, we haven't talked like this for a long time. But this has been a special day. And this evening I've been to a carol service with my daddy and I feel like a little girl again. Just thought I should tell you that. I hope you're somewhere safe and as happy as I am tonight.'

Then I fall asleep.

10
Christmas Eve 2015
This is very unusual…

My footsteps echo loudly as I walk through the hospital trying unsuccessfully to push the worrying thoughts to the back of my mind. My progress along the seemingly endless corridor is marked at intervals by the traditional signs and symbols of Christmas – bright and colourful decorations at the entrances to the various wards, a Christmas tree by one of the reception areas, the sound of carols piped through the public address system, and even a life-size montage on the wall outside the children's ward where shepherds and wise men and Mary and Joseph surround a baby lying in a crib with a golden halo above his head. But none of this makes me feel at all festive or any less concerned about what I might be about to hear.

I should have seen the consultant last week, only to be told in a phone call that he needed to delay the appointment. According to the nurse who contacted me, this was simply because he wanted additional time to 'meet with his inter-disciplinary team and review the biopsies one more time'. That, I suggested to her, could mean only bad news. She immediately attempted to put my mind at rest, assuring me that this kind of delay was not particularly uncommon and that there could be a variety of reasons for it. There was a moment towards the end of our conversation when I had a feeling that she was on the verge of sharing some additional information. But she very quickly changed tack and told me that she wasn't allowed to say any more than she'd already said, but that I shouldn't assume the worst.

At last I reach the end of the corridor and report to Mr Robertson's secretary, who explains that he's running a little behind time, invites me to take a seat and tells me without too much conviction in her voice that he shouldn't be more than fifteen minutes. I take a book from my bag and try to look unconcerned, but I manage neither to read nor to relax. In the end I give up the attempt and let my thoughts wander where they will. It always amazes me just how much goes through my head in even a few seconds and how incredibly far my mind can travel in a quarter of an hour.

I go back almost a decade to that meeting on Christmas Eve with my father in The Sailors' Rest in Avonshead. When I took him back to London with me it was with the sole intention that we'd enjoy Christmas and New Year together before I drove him to Southampton. But he never did return to his lonely flat in the city where he'd remained a stranger, hiding from his past. All through that first week he was bright and alert, interested and involved in all the festivities. I began to hope against hope that these were the first indications of a miraculous improvement in his condition. But as soon as the holiday period was over and the dark days of January began to unfold, his cough worsened and his health declined rapidly. It was as if, having fulfilled his dream of being reunited with his children, he was now ready to face the business of dying.

The evenings we spent together in those last weeks remain vivid in my mind. Sometimes we would reminisce about my childhood. Sometimes he would feel the need to apologise for his long absences from home or to confess something from his past that he'd suddenly remembered that was troubling him. Sometimes we would listen to music that he enjoyed. But mostly we would sit in the quietness of Madge's home without feeling it necessary to say anything, grateful for the unexpected opportunity to be father and daughter again. And though we invited them to visit, neither my mother nor his other two former 'wives' were willing to effect any kind of reconciliation. I understood their reluctance but I was sorry about it. I think he was genuine in his desire to seek their forgiveness for the lies he'd told and the hurt he had caused them.

Madge and I nursed him until he died peacefully on a cold day at the beginning of February. Greg and Norah came down for the funeral and we buried him in the churchyard of St Austen's. I visit his grave from time to time, saddened by his many wrong turnings and his inability for so much of his life to face reality. But I am thankful for our reconciliation and for the quality of those few weeks. That brief encounter with him felt like the completion of what had been an unfinished chapter and the opportunity to start on a new page.

It helped me to appreciate Madge in a way that I hadn't done before. Of course, I was grateful for all the help she'd given me and for the unlikely friendship we shared considering the difference in our ages. But, as younger people often do, I'd unthinkingly assumed that she'd only ever been a more youthful version of the sprightly elderly lady approaching her nineties. Now, as I deliberately took time to ask her about her past, I began to form a picture of a life that had been filled with incident and not without its own difficult times. Her eighteen-year-old fiancé, with whom she'd been passionately in love, had enlisted in the army and been killed in active service in 1943. And having lost the love of her life, she'd dealt with her grief by throwing herself into work and study and had qualified as a primary school teacher.

In her mid-thirties, when she thought she was fully reconciled to life as a single woman, she met a headmaster from a school in Durham at a national conference. Despite being separated by distance, their relationship developed to the point where they were talking about marriage, only for her to discover that he was already married with two children. He had deceived her as he'd deceived several other young single women.

It was that experience, she told me, that gave her an instinctive understanding and sympathy for my situation. For a second time she'd been hurt in love and again she discovered a measure of healing in her work. Her Christian faith became increasingly important to her, motivating her to spend the next thirty years using her teaching skills in a variety of educational projects in several African countries.

On retirement she'd returned to north London and reconnected with St Austen's, the church she'd attended as a child. A well-off benefactor who'd admired and financially supported her work while she was overseas provided her with the house she now lived in. And, being the kind of person she was, she resolved that such a gift should be shared with anyone she met who needed accommodation and a place of refuge. I wasn't the first to benefit from her hospitality, though no one else stayed as long as I did.

She carried on with her busy lifestyle, active in her church, fully involved in the life of the community, quickly dismissing with a look of disdain any suggestion that it was time for her to consider slowing down. Then, one evening in the summer of 2012 she came home, sat in her comfortable leather armchair and asked if I'd mind making her a hot drink before she went to bed.

'I must be getting old,' she chuckled. 'Can't think why I'm so tired this evening. I'll have a drink and then I think I'll have an early night.'

I remarked that she did look a little pale but gave it no more thought as I went to the kitchen to find her favourite mug and fill it with the hot chocolate she always described as her 'beverage of choice'. When I returned a few minutes later she was sitting still, her hands clasped on her lap, her eyes closed. She had the same peaceful look she always had when she stopped to take a quick nap before heading off for whatever was next on the 'to-do list' that she made for herself every morning.

I can't explain how I knew, but I realised instantly that she had died. Perhaps it was simply that she was such a vibrant personality and I was always immediately aware of her presence whenever she entered a room. But in that moment, I knew that Madge had gone. I think I had come to know her as well as anyone. At her invitation, I had moved in as her lodger, needing a place to stay for a few months until I got my life together. As things turned out, I had stayed to become her companion, a kindred spirit, even, despite the difference in our ages and my inability to commit to the kind of faith on which her life was firmly founded.

Her funeral service was one of those all too rare happenings – an occasion for celebration rather than a time for mourning. It was Ernie, one of a group of homeless men who regularly attended St Austen's drop-in centre every week, who summed her life up perfectly. He got up, walked to the front of the church just as we were about to sing the closing hymn and asked if he could be allowed to speak. The vicar was sensitive enough to ignore the murmurs of those who, smelling the alcohol on Ernie's breath, thought he should be asked to sit down in case he spoiled the dignity of the occasion. He took less than thirty seconds to say what he wanted to say.

'I just want to tell you that I'll miss her. And I won't be the only one. She was a very kind lady. She always made me and my friends feel like we really mattered.'

He turned and saluted the coffin and sat down again. Madge would have appreciated his spontaneity and his words. She never did like formality or flowery speeches.

It was only after the funeral that we learned that she'd been well aware of the precarious state of her health and had prepared for what she knew was inevitable. Somehow, among all the other things she was doing, she'd found time, without anyone else knowing, to visit a solicitor, draw up a will and arrange for the house to be sold six months after her death. She left a letter to be given to me by the lawyer when he shared the contents of her will with a group of her closest friends the day after the funeral. It was in her usual small and tidy script, unsentimental and to the point. And, practical to the last, she'd set it out just as she would have done in one of the many lists from which she worked every day.

Lori,

By the time you read this I shall be gone, but there are a few things you need to know.

1. I have a feeling you thought I was being kind to you by having you stay. The truth is that having you around has been such a help to me. It kept me from getting old and grumpy. I think I might have been gone long before this without having you around! So thank you.

2. For a while I did think of leaving you the house. But a) I've always felt that I had it in trust and that it wasn't really mine to give away; b) I think it's time you moved out of this house and made your own way in the world free from the restrictions thinking too much about me would place on you. I probably held on to you too long. I'm sorry for that; and c) there are a number of good causes I feel I ought to support in my will. I'm sure you'll understand that.

3. However, I am leaving you 25 per cent of the money from the sale of the house. That should give you enough to put down a deposit on a place that will be right for you.

4. So no more tears. I've lived life to the full despite – and, maybe more than I realise, because of – the hurts

and disappointments. (Funny how life works out like
that.) Now, you go and do likewise!
Your friend, Madge

It wasn't until I read that letter that I fully realised what a ridiculously long time I'd spent living with Madge. Ten years is a big slice of anyone's life. But I hadn't been marking time. At first I simply needed to heal from the broken relationship with Max and to come to terms with the hard truth that I couldn't cope with returning to teaching. And Madge gave me space for that. But she also knew when to bring that period to an end. She gave me just long enough to build up my strength and confidence before introducing me to Ted Burrows in early 2002.

Ted was the CEO of Kaleidoscope, an independent local radio station broadcasting throughout north London. At first, I worked part-time doing some research and covering a variety of odd jobs. Twelve months later I took my first tentative steps as a presenter. I loved the buzz of being in the studio and the challenge of trying to communicate with an audience I didn't know and couldn't see. Eventually I graduated to presenting the afternoon show from one o'clock to four o'clock every weekday.

People tell me that I'm really rather good at it. If I'm honest, I have to say that I believe they're right. And I think I know why. I very quickly learned that good radio presenters never address an audience of hundreds or thousands of listeners across the nation. The very best of them have a knack of imagining just one person sitting at home or driving their car or engaged in some repetitive job at work with the radio turned on. And they speak directly to that one person. The paradox – the miracle of radio when it's really working – is that the better they become at doing that, the more of their listeners believe themselves to be that one person. And, if you think about it, nobody has had more practice at speaking to someone they cannot see and whom they have to imagine than I have. Since I was a child, I've spent hours of my life talking to one imaginary person! And it's been the best preparation for the job I could have had. In fact, I have a little ritual I perform every day when I come off air. I sit back, fold my arms and say with a contented smile on my face, 'Well, Calippa, we've done it again. Hope you enjoyed the show.'

The combination of my passion for radio and the much-needed prod that Madge's letter gave me provided the impetus for me to move on. I left London and returned to Bristol in the middle of 2013 to take up a job presenting on West Country Radio. It feels as if I've come home. In fact, with the help of the money Madge left me, I've been able to put down a mortgage on a flat on Newman Hill from where – if I lean out of my bedroom window and turn my head to the left – I can see 17 Morley Road, my childhood home. And, to my utter delight, on sunny days the old Bath stone walls still glow with the same rich buff colour and allow me to keep on imagining that I really did grow up in a castle built of gold.

In fact, for the first two years after arriving in Bristol everything went so smoothly that it began to feel like I'd entered a fairy tale, or at least a story in which all my troubles had been left behind, the days were sunny and a 'happy ever after' ending was in prospect. My job was working out even better than I had anticipated, I'd made a number of new friends, and a year ago I met Eric. He's a police officer, a widower in his mid-forties whose wife died five years ago, leaving him with two boys to raise. We've both experienced enough of life's ups and downs to know not to rush into anything. He's a good man, his kids like me, and we've been allowing the relationship to develop at a sensible pace.

However, six months ago, I gradually became aware of something happening in my body. I've learned to live with the ongoing discomfort of the endometriosis. But this was different. I usually wear loose-fitting slacks when I'm in the studio because they're comfortable when I'm sitting still for long periods at a time. But now they began to feel tight. My first thought was that I hadn't been paying enough attention to my weight, so I watched the calories and made sure I took more exercise. It made no difference. I could see when I was getting dressed in front of the mirror in the morning that my tummy was continuing to grow. And it began to look ominously like a swelling rather than a sign of putting on a few extra pounds. I knew it was time to talk to my doctor. The initial tests for which she sent me narrowed it down to one of two possibilities. Either it was an endometrial cyst or I had ovarian cancer. It proved to be the latter.

Suddenly the fairy tale was over. I was looking at major surgery, chemotherapy and the possibility of a much-reduced life expectancy. Strange words and phrases like omentum, midline laparotomy and mucinous malignancy became a familiar part of my vocabulary. And just over three weeks ago I underwent a four-hour operation to perform a hysterectomy, to remove my ovaries, my fallopian tubes and that part of me with the funny name – the omentum – that I never knew existed. I could almost believe that it's all been a dream until I look at the enormous scar running straight up my body apart from a neat little detour around my belly button.

The really surprising thing is that, apart from the need to move very carefully to avoid setting off a spasm of pain from all that cutting and stitching, I feel remarkably well. Which only makes my fears about what I might be about to hear all the more acute.

I'm jolted out of my reminiscences and back into the present by the exasperated voice of the consultant's secretary.

'Ms Bloom, can you hear me?' She must have called my name two or three times without me realising. 'Mr Robertson will see you now. He's a on a tight schedule, remember.'

Mr Robertson, who I'm relieved to see appears to have been blessed with more patience than his secretary, smiles and invites me to take a seat. He asks me how I've been recovering from the surgery and he nods encouragingly when I tell him that the scar is healing well and that I feel much better than I expected at this early stage.

'So, Ms Bloom…' He pauses a moment, looks up from his notes and smiles again. 'Do you mind if I call you Lori? I listen to your show sometimes when I have a day off. So I almost feel that I know you.'

I tell him that, as a broadcaster, I'll take that as a compliment and that I'll be happy for him to address me by my first name. While I'm speaking, I'm trying to work out how I should read the expression on his face. He has the gravitas I would expect from someone in his position and with his responsibilities. But he doesn't have the solemn look of a man about to deliver some terrible news. I take a deep breath and wait for his verdict.

'Well, Lori, this *is* interesting,' he says, picking up the sheet of paper lying on the top of his folder. 'You were very unfortunate to have ovarian cancer at your age. It's much more common in older, post-menopausal women. But, of course, you've suffered from endometriosis all your adult life and research is telling us that that may be a contributory factor. And the tumour we removed was large, the size of a small football. But here's the good news – and I should tell you, this is very unusual – it was a very low-grade cancer. So low grade that while we will continue to monitor how you're doing, you won't need to undergo chemotherapy.'

It takes a moment for his words to sink in. When they do, I start crying and laughing at the same time. I want to say something that will express my relief and my gratitude. But the words just won't come. For no logical reason that I can think of, I start rocking backwards and forwards, inhaling and exhaling great deep breaths of sheer relief and happiness at being alive.

Mr Robertson puts his elbows on his desk, leans his chin on the backs of his clasped hands and waits until I've calmed down a little. He smiles at me before he speaks.

'It's nice to be able to give you good news. That's not always possible in my job, so I appreciate moments like this as much as my patients do. We've done our best to help you and give you the best chance of recovery. Now it's up to you to get on with life. You're still a young woman and you've got a lot of living to do. I'll be listening out for you on the radio when you're ready to get back to work.'

He gets up from his desk and shakes hands with me. I hold his hand tightly for a few seconds and whisper my thanks. As his office door closes behind me, I walk past his secretary with my head held high, ignoring what I interpret as her haughty look, and turn on to the long corridor that will take me through the hospital and back into the world outside.

When I reach the main reception area I can hear the song that's toppled Justin Bieber from the number one spot in the charts this Christmas. Somebody somewhere had the bright idea of combining Simon and Garfunkel's 'Bridge Over Troubled Water' with Coldplay's 'Fix You' and getting a choir of doctors and nurses and physiotherapists and hospital porters from the National Health Service to sing it. It sounds like an improbable match, but it works. I can't think of anything I'd rather listen to at this moment. I smile at the woman on the reception desk and start to sing along, thinking gratefully of the people I know who've built bridges over my troubled waters and helped to fix me. And for the second time in an hour, I realise I'm laughing and crying at the same time.

The early morning rain has given way to an unseasonably warm day of sunshine and clouds. I decide that I feel fit enough to walk the half mile to the bus stop rather than line up at the taxi rank. I've only gone half a dozen steps when a car pulls up beside me. It's Eric. He's still in his police officer's uniform.

'I thought I might just make it in time to pick you up,' he says, as he opens the passenger door for me to get in. 'I headed here as soon as I finished my shift. I was impatient to know how you got on. And I wanted to see if I was right about what they might tell you.'

From the moment I told him my appointment had been delayed, he'd done his best to assure me that there was a better than even chance that it would be good news. So, easing myself into the car, I tell him he was right. And for the next twenty minutes until he drops me at home, I give him a word-for-word account of what the consultant has told me. He seems even more pleased about it than I am. I watch him drive off and I experience a rush of gratitude for the good news I've received and the opportunity to share it with someone who genuinely cares about me.

By the time I've had something to eat and drink I realise that I'm really tired. But before I take a nap, I want to tell someone else about how I'm feeling and what I'm thinking. It's time to take up one of those lined blue exercise books again.

Dear Calippa

Well, I've lost a lot in these last few months. Half of my insides, for a start – with a long scar to remind me of it every day of my life from now on. And, of course, I've lost any prospect of giving birth, being a mother, watching a child to whom I have given life grow up – though even without the cancer diagnosis, the combination of the (until now) ever-present endometriosis, the all-too-swiftly passing years, and

my bad fortune and ill judgement in matters of love
have meant that I've known the chances of that were
diminishing rapidly. Those are real and painful losses.
But, for all that, as someone whose name I can't
remember once said, much still remains. I'm still alive.
I'm still a woman. I'm still Lori Bloom. There are still
people who love me. And I'm still writing these letters
to you!

And I think I'm learning more and more that living
and losing go hand in hand. To live is to lose. Some of
the people who've been important in my life have died,
many of my memories have faded, half of my life is
over. But, for good or ill, I am who I am because of all
that's happened and all I have lost.

I guess I've really known that ever since that
Christmas Eve in Kendrew's Department Store all
those years ago. You've been a constant reminder that
losing and – for want of a better word – lostness are
always there. But now I'm daring to hope that,
alongside the sadness of losing, there might be the joy
of finding something of what's been lost and even the
hope of discovering things that I never knew were
there.

Thanks for giving me some space to puzzle and muddle
my way through all this.

Your friend, Lori

I put the book back in the old sideboard, kick off my shoes
and flop onto the bed. Within seconds I'm asleep. I dream
of Christmas Eve when I was a child. I'm sitting on the
couch snuggled up to Daddy and looking at Uncle Rob
and Auntie Cheryl on the other side of the room while

Mummy finishes off some baking in the kitchen. Through the tall bay window I can see that it's beginning to snow. So I run excitedly to the porch, open the door and stand on the steps watching the big flakes drift softly to the ground. After a few minutes I begin to shiver and go back indoors. The Christmas decorations have all disappeared and there is no one in the house except me. I call out again and again, but there is no reply. I put my coat on and go wandering along Morley Road looking for the people I've lost.

11
Christmas Eve 2019
What's your most memorable
Christmas…

Eric won't be home until late afternoon, so I make sure that the boys know what there is for lunch before I set off for work. They're really old enough to look after themselves now. A gentle reminder, however, that there are things that definitely must *not* be eaten before Christmas Day won't go amiss. The amount of food that two healthy young males can remove from a fridge in one afternoon still takes me by surprise.

Despite all the normal challenges of raising teenage boys, we get on well together and they've accepted me without too much difficulty. It was my concerns about how well I'd adapt to being a stepmother and how they'd respond to me that made me take so long to accept Eric's proposal of marriage. But two years ago, following his persistent pleas – only slightly tongue-in-cheek – that I was the only one who could save him from the fate of a lonely old age and constant indigestion from a diet of takeaway curries, I agreed to become his wife.

I close the front door and set off for the studio feeling pleased with life in general and grateful in particular for the joys of family life that I thought had eluded me for ever.

I'm pleased that Phillie Matthews is already in the studio when I arrive for my afternoon show. We have half an hour to go over things together before I go live on air at one o'clock. I love working with Phillie as my producer and I've got to know her and something of her story. She joined West Country Radio as a producer six months ago after twenty years with one of London's biggest commercial radio stations. Like me, moving to Bristol has been something of a homecoming for her. She spent her childhood and youth here after arriving in this country from the Solomon Islands as a toddler. Her biological parents had died in a house fire when she was only a baby and she'd been adopted by a Bristol couple who brought her to the UK when they returned from a three-year project with a Christian mission agency.

She's a dark-skinned, bright-eyed, white-haired woman in her late forties with a sharp mind, a larger-than-life personality, a wicked sense of humour and an infectious laugh that makes anyone who works with her feel better even on the dreariest of days. Just a smile and a reassuring nod from her through the studio window can spur me on when I feel myself running low on energy as the clock moves towards four o'clock in the afternoon.

Today there's a lot to fit in to the three hours ahead of me. But, as always, Phillie has everything in hand; the running order is right in front of me, and by one o'clock we're ready to roll. I get that same tingle of nervous anticipation every time I hear the station promos and ads just after the news on the hour. And then there's the familiar release of tension and the addictive adrenaline rush that comes over me as I speak those first words into the microphone and get the show going.

'Good afternoon. It's the 24th of December – as if you needed me to tell you that – and you're listening to *Afternoon Sounds* on West Country Radio with me, Lori Bloom. I'm here right through until four o'clock with a special festive menu of good conversation, a generous helping of stories from across the region, a side-serving of hints and helps to get your Christmas off to the best possible start, and all washed down with the refreshing tang of sparkling music I know you'll love. And I can't think of a better aperitif to start the show and get you into the true Christmas spirit than the most surprising but most deserving hit of many a year.'

It flashes though my mind that my lifelong obsession with the UK's popular music charts must have been a sign that I was always destined for a career in radio. I can hear the smile in my voice as I continue.

'Oh yes, it's the song that's beaten Stormzy, Lewis Capaldi and Wham! to the number one spot. The first act to claim consecutive Christmas number ones in more than twenty years. And all the proceeds from its sales going to a great cause that'll provide healthy food for families in need not only at Christmas but throughout the year. You know what I'm talking about. You know it's got to be LadBaby and the splendidly crazy "I Love Sausage Rolls"!'

I deliver that last sentence with all the panache of a circus ringmaster and sit back with a look of triumph as Phillie fades up the music. It's always a relief to get another show under way and I'm always excited by the challenge of ad libbing my way through the next three hours. Phillie gives me the thumbs up and I hear her voice in my headphones saying, 'It's gonna be a good one today, Lori.'

It turns out to be exactly that – a good show, fast-moving and thoroughly entertaining, judging from the encouraging calls and messages we receive. I follow the opening music track with an interview over the phone with a spokeswoman for the Trussell Trust, the charity that supports a network of food banks and that will benefit from the sales of LadBaby's chart-topping single. The stories she relates are a reminder that this will be a difficult Christmas for so many people in Britain today.

I lighten the mood a little in the second hour by talking to a man in his eighties who's been employed as Santa Claus in the toy department of a store in Taunton every year since 1999 and who has some hilarious tales to tell of the ways he's discovered to get his own back on ungrateful or badly behaved children. I'm not surprised that he prefers to remain anonymous. We have thirty pupils from a nearby school crowded into the studio to sing some traditional carols and to tell us what they're hoping to find in their stockings tomorrow morning. And Chef André, whose Bristolian accent belies his French name and whose breath suggests that he might have been imbibing the brandy he suggests we use, comes over from the *Hotel Culinaire* to tell us how to make the perfect sauce to accompany the Christmas pudding.

But it's in the last hour of the show that we make the all-too-elusive transition from being a good show to becoming really compelling radio. It begins with Jo Burton, our roving reporter out on the streets of Bristol, stopping people and asking them to recall their most memorable Christmas. Their answers range from the hilarious to the deeply moving. One woman confesses to the time when she forgot to put the turkey in the oven and the family ended up eating beans on toast for Christmas dinner. A middle-aged man still sounds embarrassed by a mix-up, to which no one in the family has owned up even after twenty years, when he opened the present with his name on it in front of his young children only to reveal what he sensitively describes as 'a rather naughty item of lady's intimate apparel'. And a tearful elderly woman recounts an unforgettable wartime memory of her brother, who'd been listed as missing in action and was presumed dead somewhere in France, turning up on the doorstep late on Christmas Eve to the unrestrained joy of a grateful family.

Just as we get to the end of that interview I get a message from Phillie, 'Don't do a link, Lori. I know the perfect record to follow this.' And, as one of Bristol's older citizens ends her touching story and a thousand listeners reach for a tissue, I hear the unmistakable voice of Bing Crosby with a tear-jerking standard from the 1940s that I barely know and would certainly never have thought of: 'I'll Be Home for Christmas'. It's a perfect radio moment and it's all down to Phillie Matthews' quick thinking and her almost encyclopaedic knowledge of the station's music library. This time it's my turn to give the thumbs up.

As the track ends, I'm just about to talk to Jo Burton for thirty seconds and allow her to sign off before I get on with the rest of the show. But Jo's not ready to leave yet. Totally unscripted and entirely off the cuff, she fires a question at me.

'So, Lori. All these nice people hurrying home with their last-minute shopping have been kind enough to stop and tell me about their most memorable Christmas while you've been sat there in that comfortable studio letting us do all the hard work out here. So come on, be fair. What about you? What's your most memorable Christmas?'

The question takes me completely by surprise and I commit the unforgiveable sin for a radio presenter – I can't think of what to say in reply. The silence probably lasts no more than a second or two, though it feels much longer as my mind scans my memories, good and bad, of past Christmases: seeing those disturbing photos of my father with another woman; learning the truth about his bizarre life of fantasy, deceit and crime; my first innocent kiss by the side of Wythmere; that dismal and desolate Christmas following Reuben's drowning; Leroy Williams' question on the busy Holloway Road about what I believed that has niggled at me ever since; handing out carol sheets and candles with Madge Timmins at St Austen's; seeing my father again after so many years in The Sailor's Rest in Avonshead; the overwhelming relief of the consultant's assurance that my cancer wasn't terminal.

I can see Phillie staring at me through the studio window with her eyes wide open and a look that screams louder than any words could: 'Get on with it, Lori!'

I start to speak without knowing what I'm going to say.

'Well, Jo, you've caught me on the hop there. But since you ask...'

It's only as the words begin to form that I realise there's only one Christmas I can talk about. One that has stayed with me longer than any other and had such an impact on who I am. One that I've only ever shared with a few close friends.

'Well, since you ask...'

I pause again, still uncertain if I'm being wise in sharing something on air that's so important to me, but feeling at the same time that I've been ambushed and there's no escape. I swallow quickly and continue.

'Since you ask, my most memorable Christmas was way back in 1976. I wasn't quite four years old.' The words come slowly, but I know there's no turning back now. 'It's a memory of a little girl I never saw, a little girl whose name I probably misheard and that my parents always thought I'd made up, a little girl who's probably long forgotten the incident. It was in Kendrew's Department Store. It isn't there any longer but older listeners will remember it. I was coming down the escalator with my mother and an announcement came over the tannoy saying that there was a little girl with curly blonde hair at reception who was lost and who was crying for her mummy and daddy. The thought of that little girl, who I guessed must be around my own age, looking up into the faces of strangers, touched my heart. I wanted to go straight to reception and hold her hand, talk to her. But my mother was in a hurry to get home. She told me that there was nothing to worry about and that her mummy and daddy would definitely hear the message and find her. I'm sure she was right. But that moment has stayed with me all through the years. I still think of that little girl, and in my mind... well, I guess she's lost forever.'

I realise that I'm actually beginning to get weepy and I try to pull myself together. This is hardly what you'd expect from an experienced broadcaster. I can hear Phillie's voice through my headphones.

'Why don't you tell them the name you thought you heard?' She sounds a little emotional too. 'It's a great story. Go on, don't stop.'

The professional broadcaster part of me kicks in. Never miss an opportunity to grab your listener's attention. If my story's having that kind of impact on someone as worldly wise as Phillie, I think to myself, it must be having an effect on the audience. I decide to go for broke and tell all.

'And the name of that little girl, the name I thought I heard that day, the name I've never forgotten – even though it sounds ridiculous to my adult mind when I say it aloud now – is Calippa Cumberland.' I think I've weathered the emotional storm and allow myself to smile at my embarrassment. 'I know... *Calippa Cumberland*! Sounds silly, I know. And, since I'm telling you more about myself than you probably want to know, I might as well admit that she not only became my imaginary friend through most of my childhood, but even now, when I need to unburden myself, I think of her. I keep a kind of journal of what's going on in my life. Anything important.

Anything that's troubling me. But I write in the form of a letter addressed to *Dear Calippa*. Who knows? Maybe I'll meet her some day. Maybe I'll be able to show them to her and she can read them.'

The clock on the wall is showing that there's less than thirty minutes until the end of the show. And there's quite a bit more to fit in before we come up to the news at four o'clock. I need to keep things moving and I'm just about to introduce a three-minute music track when I notice that Phillie isn't sitting in her usual seat on the other side of the glass. I'm trying to work out why she's not there when I hear the soft whoosh of the studio door opening and Phillie herself comes in and sits down by the mic opposite me. Her face is beaming and her eyes are glistening and I'm not sure whether she's laughing or crying or doing both at the same time. Before I can say another word, she puts her finger in front of her lips to tell me to stay quiet, points to herself and begins to speak into the mic in front of her.

'Now you won't recognise my voice,' she says, addressing the listeners. 'I'm Phillie Matthews, I'm the producer of *Afternoon Sounds* and it's my job to stay on the other side of the mic and make sure everything's running smoothly for Lori to get on with the show. But when I explain why I'm interrupting the proceedings today, I think you'll understand. Lori's just shared with you a vivid memory from childhood, and I want to tell you about something that stands out just as clearly from my childhood. But first of all, I need to tell you a little of my background.'

I still can't work out what's happening, why Phillie's sitting there talking about *her* childhood. She's always happy for her presenters to have the limelight. But she keeps going, quickly sketching in the details of her earliest years – her birth in the Solomon Islands, the loss of her parents and her adoption by English missionaries who brought her to England and to their home city of Bristol.

'So now,' she goes on, 'I come to the part of my story that I want you and Lori to listen to very carefully. You can imagine how strange and even frightening everything was to me, a little three-year-old in a new country and a big city. That's why I remember so vividly my very first Christmas Eve here. It was 1976 and my parents took me to Kendrew's Department Store…'

Suddenly I have a sense that, apart from the sound of Phillie's voice, everything has gone quiet. So quiet that I can hear my heart beating. For a moment everything feels distant and I have to concentrate on what Phillie's saying.

'I don't know how it happened, but I got separated from my parents. Some kind person heard me crying and took me to the reception desk. I can still see those faces looking down at me. I can still remember the panic I felt. I can still remember them asking my name. I can still hear them calling it out over the booming loudspeakers. I can still remember the relief when my parents came rushing into the reception area to collect me. And, as you can imagine, it was a story that we remembered every Christmas Eve. Much to my embarrassment as I got older, I might say.'

I'm struggling to believe what I'm hearing. Is this just a bizarre coincidence? Surely Phillie wouldn't make a joke like this at my expense, would she?

'I can see your incredulous expression, Lori,' she says, a smile spreading across her face. 'I think I'd better fill you in on some details. Phillie, as I've been known since I started school here in Bristol, is short for Philippa. And the couple who adopted me were Jim and Mary Sutherland. So I became *Philippa Sutherland*. And that's the name that was announced over the tannoy that afternoon. The name that you must have heard as *Calippa Cumberland*. So, Lori Bloom, I think I'm your long-lost friend.'

'B-b-but you can't be,' I stammer over my words as I try to comprehend what I've just heard. 'I distinctly remember that the little girl who was lost had blonde hair. And you're...'

I can't think how to say what I want to say without it sounding rude or politically incorrect or whatever.

'It's alright, you can say it. You mean I couldn't be the blonde-haired little girl whose name you heard. Because I'm black!' Now Phillie's smile has become a laugh that means she has to compose herself and take a deep breath before she can continue. 'But remember I'm from the Solomon Islands. And one of the interesting things about us Solomon Islanders is that, while we have some of the darkest skin outside Africa, about 10 per cent of us have blonde hair. Nobody's quite sure why. One theory is that it's inherited from early European traders who came to the islands. Other experts think it's got something to do with a diet that's rich in fish. Or maybe it's a genetic thing.

Whatever it is, it means that it's not uncommon, especially in childhood, for a Solomon Islander to have blonde hair.'

Now I'm experiencing a moment that every radio presenter dreads. I'm completely dumbstruck. Fortunately, Phillie has no difficult filling in for my silence.

'And though I'm now a middle-aged, white-haired woman, I was certainly a blonde-haired little girl. In fact, the description the man at the reception gave of me that afternoon was one of the reasons the incident was celebrated as much as it was remembered in my family. There was still a fair bit of prejudice around in those days. I'd been referred to more than a few times as "that dark child" or "that little coloured girl". And my parents were delighted to hear their daughter spoken of without any mention of the colour of my skin. They actually wrote a letter to the Kendrew's employee who made that announcement to thank him for how he described me. So, Lori, I don't think there's any room for doubt. You've found me at last.'

Now I don't even make any attempt to speak as the tears run down my face. Fortunately, Phillie has the presence of mind to make sure that the technician on the desk is playing the next music track before she stands up and walks across the studio to embrace me.

'I can't believe this,' I say through my tears. 'I really have found you after all these years. You've no idea how many one-sided conversations I've had with you or how many letters I've written to you. But they're all in my collection of lined blue exercise books. I'll let you read them if you can ever be bothered.'

'Well, I'm glad you've found me and so grateful that you've cared about that little lost girl all these years. And I'd love to read them.' She pulls a couple of tissues from the pocket of her slacks and puts them in my hand. 'But we've got a show to complete. So I'm going back to my place and you need to get on with it. You're a professional broadcaster, remember.'

At first, I'm not sure how I'm going to get through the next twenty minutes to the end of the show. But I needn't have worried. It turns into a phone-in as I read out the emails and texts and answer the calls that come flooding in from grateful listeners who are unanimous in their opinion that this has been the best *Afternoon Sounds* we've ever done. One woman in her nineties has me sniffling again when she says that it's years since she had such a good cry while 'listening to the wireless' and that the thought of me finding the little girl who was lost in Kendrew's Department Store all those years ago has made her Christmas.

With only minutes left before the news on the hour, it's time for me to introduce Andy Lewis, who leads the church just a few hundred yards along the street from the studio. Andy's one of a group of faith leaders who know how to talk on the radio without using pious jargon that we call on to close the show whenever it's one of the great religious festivals. And, this being Christmas Eve, he's the man to reflect on the day from a Christian perspective. He sits down at the mic opposite me where Phillie was sitting just twenty minutes ago. He always arrives in good time and he always has his script carefully typed so that he doesn't waste a word and doesn't take a second more than he's been allotted. But now he pushes his notes to one side as he leans into the mic.

'I always enjoy talking to you on *Afternoon Sounds*. But after what we've just heard in the last half hour, you're probably not sure if you really need a clergy person like me to tie it all up with a nice religious bow. And I agree with you. Lori's concern for her long-lost friend says so much about this season we're celebrating. What an illustration of the power of imagination. A brief announcement of the plight of a little lost girl was enough for her to form a picture that's stayed with her for forty years. And I think the reason Christmas has such a hold on us, whether we call ourselves religious or not, is that the plight of a baby shut out of a crowded inn and born in a stable takes hold of our imagination in a similar way. And a bit like Lori, if you allow it to take hold of your heart, you can't help wondering and asking what happened to that infant.'

Andy pauses for a moment, and I wonder if he's going to stop there. He looks at me and glances quickly at Phillie, who's smiling and nodding in agreement on the other side of the glass. That seems to give him the inspiration he needs to continue with his impromptu reflection.

'If you do that, you might well find you arrive at a similar place to Lori today. The truth is, we all know what it's like to lose people we love and things that matter to us. And we all know what it's like to feel lost ourselves. I do the job I do, not because I've got a special religious gene that sets me apart from normal folk or because I'm blessed with an extra measure of faith denied to others. No, I do it because I know what it's like to lose and to be lost, and I'm persuaded that the child born on that first Christmas became the man in whose presence lost people are found and lost causes are rescued. I'm so convinced that, just as Lori had conversations with Calippa Cumberland, I have conversations with Him. That could just be my imagination, of course...'

He pauses and looks at me again and I wonder if he wants me to come in and take us to the end of the show. But before I can speak, he leans back into the mic and says in a quiet but clear voice, 'Or it could be that, a bit like in Lori's story, my God-given imagination has led me to a surprising but wonderful friendship. I guess we all have to discover that and decide that for ourselves. Have a wonderful Christmas.'

It's almost four on the studio clock and we need to go straight to the news. For the first time in my career as a broadcaster, I'm not annoyed by the fact that I don't get to have the last word and round off the show. I'm not sure I'd know what to say.

It's been one of the best days of my life and I need to make sense of what this all means. Whether all I've been telling you is nothing more than the work of my overactive imagination. Whether it means anything at all. Whether what's happened is nothing more than coincidence. Whether it's a pointer to the deep truth at the heart of the universe that Andy believes he's discovered. Like he says, I guess we all have to discover it and decide for ourselves.

And, of course, I really *can* talk to Calippa Cumberland about it this Christmas...

Also by Chick Yuill:

Seventy-five-year-old, green-fingered Albert Stridemore's carefully ordered life has been unchanged for years. Content to live alone and diligently work his allotment, he safely buries the past as he turns the soil. But with the arrival of the coronavirus and lockdown, he finds himself digging up more than just potatoes in the spring.

With time to think and an unexpected new acquaintance in the attractive widow Penny Finch, Albert is compelled to revisit past betrayals, even as his eyes are opened to a generous and richer world in the present.

And when injustice is exposed as the virus strikes close to home, Albert is thrust into a new role and makes the most unexpected discoveries…

Instant Apostle, 2020, ISBN 978-1-909728-33-2

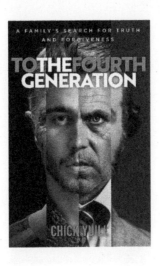

Zander Bennings' writing has brought him a lifestyle his parents and grandparents could never have imagined. But when he is confronted with the cold reality that his success is built upon a lie, he is plunged into a desperate search for truth and forgiveness.

Delving into his family's past, through the battlefields of World War One and down the three generations before his own, he discovers that the men of his family have each been forced to embark upon this same unsettling quest.

Tracing their lives, and those of the women who held the family together, Zander discovers the search is not in vain, and that while family ties can be broken, they can never be truly severed – even to the fourth generation.

Instant Apostle, 2020, ISBN 978-1-909728-26-4

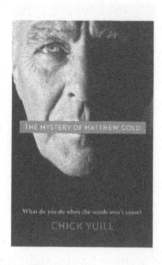

Meet Matthew Gold: wealthy, successful and secure – but totally alone. Afflicted from childhood by a crippling stammer, words have been his greatest problem. But, as his talent as a writer of detective fiction emerges, words become his greatest passion. He might struggle to speak, but on the pages of his novels his slick-talking private eye knows all the answers and can always find the words to illuminate every mystery.

But what happens when life itself becomes a mystery you cannot solve? What do you say and what can you do when words come to an end?

Instant Apostle, 2019, ISBN 978-1-909728-65-3

When the caretaker of St Peter's finds that the church has been broken into early on the Saturday morning after Christmas and that the elderly intruder is still in the building and kneeling at the communion rail, no one is quite sure what to do.

But the confusion caused by the sudden arrival of this unexpected visitor is as nothing compared to the impact of his continuing presence on the church and the town. As his identity becomes clear and his story unfolds, long-hidden truths emerge, and life in Penford can never be quite the same again...

Instant Apostle, 2018, ISBN 978-1-909728-87-5

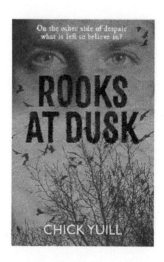

On the other side of despair
what is left to believe in?

ROOKS
AT DUSK

CHICK YUILL

Where can a man find grace when he no longer believes? Ray Young has been married for almost thirty years. But his once vibrant faith, like his marriage, is steadily fading, and relations with his only son Ollie are increasingly strained.

Facing this looming crisis of faith, Ray begins an affair, only for Ollie to discover his father's infidelity. Confronted by his actions, Ray has one chance to rescue the life that is crumbling around him. But when tragedy strikes, it seems all hope of redemption is gone…

Instant Apostle, 2017, ISBN 978-1-909728-65-3